the
Third
Body

the Third Body

Hélène Cixous

NORTHWESTERN UNIVERSITY PRESS
EVANSTON, ILLINOIS

Northwestern University Press
www.nupress.northwestern.edu

Originally published in French in 1970 under the title *Le troisième corps*
by Editions Grasset, Paris. Copyright © Hélène Cixous, represented by
Myriam Diocaretz Foreign Rights Agency. English translation copyright © 1999
by Hydra Books/Northwestern University Press. Published 1999 by arrangement
with Hélène Cixous. All rights reserved.

First paperback printing 2009

Printed in the United States of America
10 9 8 7 6 5 4 3 2 1

ISBN 978-0-8101-2654-1

The Library of Congress has cataloged the original, hardcover edition as follows:

Cixous, Hélène, 1937–
      [Troisième corps. English]
      The third body / Hélène Cixous ; translated from the French
      by Keith Cohen.
        p. cm.
      ISBN 0-8101-1687-1 (cl. : alk. paper)
      I. Title. II. Title: 3rd body.
   PQ2663.I9T713 1999
   843'.914—dc21   99-27406
                                              CIP

for a long time I closed my eyes when he would leave, and I kept my eyes closed when we made love. Back in those years when he was so close or so far away, I would often lose myself in an ageless non-place where I no longer felt anything. Sometimes I was overcome by sleep. Then I would dream that he was leaving, I could see him leaving in minute detail, and this detailed departure grated the flesh of my eyes so minutely that my grief from the knowledge that he was leaving and my grief at seeing him leave crushed my bones and lacerated my skin, and yet I saw him gone, his back dripping with blood. I could see him leaving. Then the arms, the legs, which are mine when he's here, would rip off and fall upon him. I wouldn't try to hold him back. But he is in my flesh, and he is in my eyes, and he is the marrow of my bones. By leaving he drew me away from myself, the self that wasn't leaving with him except by means of the immovable in me, and if I'd had my eyes open, I would have seen his back dripping with blood. You are the marrow of my bones. You are flesh to me. One of us felt we were dying with each departure. One of us knew that it wasn't death but a pain as vivid and complete as the body of the one departing, that of the one staying behind, identical to that body, a body pained

1

by violent absence. The body and the pain knew each other, and by being mixed together resembled one another, were named by the same words. A new homonymy was born for them, through his voice or mine, without distinguishing: "My arm!" also meant my arm hurts (yours, mine). "Oh my mouth, my lips, my teeth, and my tongue!" meant rescue my mouth which is for you and moisten my dry lips, and separate my tongue from my teeth that are biting it so it won't cry out yet, oh my mouth, your lips, the tongue that comes to me from you all the better to accuse us of each still having these lips, those lips, while in fact for a long time we've had only one tongue to question and answer. With each departure: we had to believe the unbelievable, do the impossible, separate the marrow from its bones, yet keep walking, letting the blood flow here, the heart beat there. And keep seeing the blood, the heart, and the marrow in the bones. Keep having in our eyes the flowing, the beating, the pounding.

There was a week in October, like a long, invincible arrival, so strong, so prolonged, so certain, so vibrant because of all the senses getting satisfaction, that everything could have changed— did change by all appearances. An unexpected week though. Nothing had foretold it, we hadn't prepared it, we had neither expected nor imagined it. At least neither one of us had had the least hint or advance sign of it. This time came upon us after several years, numerous months, innumerable days, all different, each with its name, its number, its special flavor, and what they all had in common was that they ended with a departure, and each time there was this blood and this terror in greater or lesser quantity. They would come to an end sometimes in an hour, sometimes in a minute, sometimes in several units of pain (hours, days, nights, weeks). Through a door, at a subway, round a bend in the avenue, backward. The end must be pulled off like a bandage: a quick pulling off, abrupt, a brief burning, just the right brusqueness. There were pitiful brutalities between us. He zeroed in on my disappearances: I was supposed to refine my method down to the tiniest gesture, to the point of inimitably mastering a suicide with no death; I knew how to disappear so deftly that he couldn't believe his eyes. I arrived at such perfection in the end that my disappearance disappeared. The features of my disappearance expressed a resolute indifference toward external events; the eye that looked straight into his eye showed a piercing, extraordinary look and, etching itself on his willing retina, proceeded with a rapid folding back of thoughts upon themselves. In short, my disappearance was foreseen because of a final look in which it was established that everything was in order, then it *was,* but it couldn't be seen, for it absorbed itself. T.t. was convinced that he was the locus of my disappearance, and I often experienced it as such: but it was only in the instant that preceded my reappearance that I recognized, by the form of its walls and the odor of its tissues, the thoracic cage in which I quivered, and that scarcely lasted, for as soon as I opened my eyes, my disappearance had disappeared, cut out from the memory of my senses as utterly as a dream.

That year of Octobers was triumphant; we kept on arriving, our arrival spread right into each other's arms, reverberated, ricocheted, while the disappearances were executed so remarkably that we didn't even feel them: we knew that they were over only because of the spreading, sonorous, intoxicating, perfumed, multiple arrival, fed by itself, stimulated by all our muscles together, but savored slowly. And not a drop of blood. We had discovered the secret of uninterrupted bringing to life. We sailed through time as though it were God the mother, a comic figure, protectress, little old woman, ambitious, harmless, foiled. Without hurrying, *festina lente*. Passing by, T.t. cut the false cords that had threatened to strangle me while I was resigned to the permanence of their knots, as they were old and had appeared to me irremovable. And there was nothing, no reason for this revolution, no visible sign. O adorable Plenitude of that Monday pregnant with a Tuesday that gave us Wednesday that opened onto Thursday that left us off around Friday that dropped us into the dazzling light of Saturday. Lofty days, bets taken, forces in alternation. Sometimes his joy preceded mine, other times I took the first step of the day. Eyes finally came to me, and those eyes were naked. With those eyes I saw at first only his eyes; as strange as it may seem, I had never really seen his eyes, their scope and their strength and their radiance, so precisely. Each of his looks is another look and a look and one other look, and I don't have enough eyes to see you. I had never gone into his eyes, and it was impossible to go into them without putting them out: it was forbidden depth, and his eyes had no voice that, rising from his inner depths, could have reassured me, they had a clarity, a transparence that showed there must have been a way of seeing him in them. What face, what body awaited me there? Could I look at his brain as though I saw it through the signs of his eyes? My new eyes, as I've said, were penetrating. They were swallowed up everywhere with such a huge appetite to see inside that through the swallowing up were constructed all these curved, hollow cavities that we use as beds, explorable dens, nearly unknown till now, for we had never dreamed of seeing ourselves there; I myself had always shut my eyes each time a hollow appeared, and each time I fell, clearly, into the blackness of fear.

Everything was gotten over, cut through, let go of, launched, scattered, Saturday October morning, October, beyond September beyond August, since we had written *Out-of-bounds* years ago, anti-month, a hole in the year, when we couldn't see ourselves. With all these outs we could have made a monster year, without stars, its eyes bulging, which we could have saved for later. Paris was out because of the light one Saturday, because of the color of the daylight, true blue, the length of the avenues walked in every direction, reversed, contradicted, unruly, cunning. We ran, we watched each other run. We got dressed, we watched each other get dressed in the mirrors of the dressers, he taller, I shorter, but with the same skin inside out, peeled back, hidden, revealed. Painting each other's, inscribing it, touching it. Spend, take, take, take, we take everything, take take, we flare up, we get fresh air, we take the the, take take take, all the images we cut them out, we try them. It takes; joy comes from deep down. It took. Then we'll see the apartment, O Happy Day. We count the squares of glass in the apartment, there are 365, that's normal. We'll take it. We've gotten help from numbers for a long time.

*a*t noon, October, Saturday, broken, seeded, like yesterday and yesterday's yesterday, it's so hot that flies are born. A bee comes into the room. The sky darkens, in every sense of the word. My disappearance progresses like a dream figure, and as I stand next to him we watch it come show itself to be done away with by us. It comes from now, not knowing where to place itself. Unhurriedly, for it is already the shadow of itself and it does not know itself where to set down and it buzzes in the room where Saturday is pregnant with Monday. Finally I am going to dare to catch a glimpse of my body at loss, my body bloody with departures. He is tall and slender, with black wavy hair, his head bent forward, the curve of his eyelids is not mine: he's the one who looks down at the path.

Side by side, and we look at it; I hear you smile, my cheek, my temple let me know. We are happy because we are no longer members of the everyday. What comes toward us with a step that doesn't know where to set down is a dream figure in broad daylight. But there where we do not sleep there is no daylight to hold us back or to trick us into taking it for a model of forever.

We grow, by the gaze of one another.

The left foot put out in front, and the right ready to follow, touches the ground only with the tip of its toes, while its
sole and heel rise up almost vertically. This movement of the
disappearance on the point of disappearing holds us back,
seduces us. Today distance gives us the beauty of our forms
seen from farther and farther away. My eyes rock it at twenty
yards, close in upon it at ten yards, spread over it at five
yards, and at three yards caress it with a single wide-open
caress. There. Don't move, don't move, my eyes are filled and
open. Eyes filled with your flesh, bellies lit up. Come forward, slowly, no, stop, yes, come forward, softly, farther, farther ah I'm going to disappear, you get bigger, I see no more
than a bit of you, soon I see the disappearance walking, but
no matter then, I see it through the breast where I am. The
movement that he saw when my eyes drew near him
expressed at once the agile freedom of a young woman walking and a repose sure of itself, a non-objection, which gave
her, by combining a sort of suspended flight with a steady
gait, the bare charm of beings unafraid of passing away.

That's what I say to T.t. then: my disappearance has the
calm gait of something unafraid of passing away. These words
were not separated. They had been entrusted to me in a single full, polite sentence, which I at once passed on to T.t. On
them (these words), my disappearance takes place.

I no longer remember the passing.

That evening, L. comes to bring me various books, difficult to find before the advent, and I can't help telling her the

story of the fly, which seems to me to symbolize nicely our being together, during a morning discussion, before our trip across town, which was about my difficulty controlling my gestures made just as I fall asleep—a difficulty that had gotten surprisingly worse in the past weeks. In fact, I had just given in to an unusual act, banal no doubt, yet striking because of the moment it had thrust itself upon me: I woke up with a start in the dark bedroom alive with imperceptible oscillations. My watch showed an hour that started up the next day in me. So I immediately phoned up L., to whom I'd made a friendly pledge that had turned this act into a ritual. A soft voice answered, putting questions to me patiently, without surprise, with a reassuring rising and falling in her voice, asking me gently who I was and what was happening. The first time, I had experienced an emotion all the more violent because, at the very moment I realized my mistake, I was convinced not only that I knew the voice, but also that she too guessed something or other, hence her calmness and concern, and yet I could attach no name, no face to this voice, but, swallowed up into an eager silence, listening, searching, I heard her at last stop speaking, as if reluctantly, but without bitterness. I was not able to say who I was or to find out who she was. I was the one who hung up; she waited. I felt a wave of mad love for her, a certitude that my mistake was a screen for some truth. But I didn't know which number I had dialed for her. And I had been mistaken, truly, about what time it was; it was night—daylight and the time to get started were still way off, and when they caught up with me I didn't know anything anymore. I remembered that I had loved, in another life at once far off and close at hand, a woman no doubt older than myself who knew everything, or more precisely a woman who loved me "no matter what."

The following night, a new call: I am called on to call, but this time, luckily or unluckily, I do not hear the patient voice; I hear the ringing of the telephone that cuts through the skin of my sleep with a sudden violence and gives a shove to my consciousness the way an undesirable is thrown out the door. As I fall I see myself dialing the number, my trembling index finger gets halfway through, but then I crash into a rocky awakening that interrupts the conspicuous gesture. What remain in me are the first five numbers and the hope that she didn't pick up the receiver because maybe she didn't hear anything, so it's as though I hadn't done anything. 53333. I did her no harm. I remember her gentleness. I didn't tell her who I was because I didn't know who I was, and then when I explain to T.t. that I'm afraid of hurting someone I love during sleep (to unmask, to kill, to bring down, to denounce—all these demons are in me in the infinitive of threat), I read in his eyes, turned full on me down to the last eyelash, that he knows the number of the patient voice. We are sitting cross-legged when I say 5, 3, 3, 3, 3, and I repeat it, being surprised to hear only at that instant the multiplicity of threes. I'm saying this to myself—533, 33, 33, 33—it happened in 533, there are 533 rungs in Jacob's ladder, I'm 3 years old, I'm 33 years old, he's 53 years old minus 3 years, it wasn't a bee, it was a fly that hovered in front of us at the height of 33 above mother-level [au-dessus du niveau de la mère], above her who spoke to me once. And with that I am struck with a presentiment: she's drawing near; it seems to me, I say, that the telephone is going to call me, I am possessed of an excitement analogous to that which I feel upon going back over my dreams, my heart moves, lodges on the right, is nailed down in the center, swells.

With mouth open, eyes open, hands open, as though I were expected at mass. The fly goes in by my mouth. Winged host, little bitty p . . . , what are you doing? I could have brought it round and made it come back up, coughed, spat, brought it back up, with the same force, effortlessly, that it had when it landed on me, but it was so small, and what happens to us is so great. I was reluctant to interrupt the flow of our happy story, in which we were touching on the outer limits, getting close to all those mysteries, in order to announce this undeniable yet insignificant fact that I had swallowed a fly. An inaccurate and not just impertinent statement, moreover: it was not an ordinary fly, it was smaller and more agitated than what I call a fly, and the fineness of coloring on its wings made it akin to those tiny almond-green moths, truncated dragon-flies an eighth of an inch long that are so sanctimonious in September. And then I wasn't sure I swallowed it, it had sim-ply disappeared, at a moment when it was so close to my mouth that there was no other place it could have disappeared into, it was just not outside my mouth anymore, as in a sleight-of-hand disappearance. I felt right afterward an imper-ceptible irritation around my uvula, which made me come to the conclusion that it had passed by there. I wasn't going to make a big deal out of it or allow a gnat the time for a single phrase. I swallowed. How familiar and yet singular was my delight upon hearing T.t.'s cheerful voice saying to me, like a dog on a leash, joyous, panting: wasn't it 533-33-13? Yes, yes, 13, that's it, that's it; who is it? He tells me effusively with the passion of a game of passion, and I'm filled with dread, with cold, I don't know; what I hear stops me in my tracks, chills me, I can't help going back to my initial suspicions, and fear-ing the incursion within me of the Unmasking demon, my joy is now mixed with shame, I think in fear, mixed with the

10

scarcely tangible bit of a question that's no longer willing to be popped. But the important thing is *his* attitude: in fact, he's happy. No emissary from the netherworld will ever diminish his joy. What comes our way, whatever its origin, becomes a good thing as it draws near us. He is happy, he assails me with all kinds of strange little questions, charmed accomplice of the Unmasker, to the point that I too marvel at the act whose stakes really are the difference between life and death, between absolute knowledge and absolute ignorance.

★

Afterward we burst straight into Paris and picked up all our reflections from the dresser mirrors, but that's where the fly comes back in. At first you feel a slight irritation, a yen to scratch if only you could reach that point of your gullet; you clear your throat. I wondered if it could have "settled" on some obscure, purple cornice of my throat. Then everything picks up speed: first my throat dries out fairly fast, my voice, which has become chalky, cracks, a fire is set. I can no longer speak now except by signs, can hardly breathe. Drink. Diagnosis of a stupid death. Coca-Cola. Lesson: the laws of arbitrariness. A critic said that my last book "swarmed [*fourmillement*] with precise notations about the most everyday life-events." One shouldn't say in a book that one has already written a book. There is, there ought to be, a law aimed at this type of adultery. I cite this phrase because of the high incidence of germs of meaning in it, at least to my ear. So the fact that it came and whispered to me seems to me entirely to the point. First because of the mysterious syntagma "the most everyday life-events" (the least everyday, and the more or less everyday, and all the beds of life that I don't remember having slept in). Then because of ants [*fourmis*]

11

being associated with flies and earwigs. Ants swarm outside, they come at you from the outside. When you get ants on your limbs, they clear out all by themselves after a certain period of time. There is nothing more repugnant than those columns of little black ants that climbed up onto my sickbed several years ago, silent, so rapid that their movement was fluvial, an aggression divided up to infinity which aimed at each of the cells of my epidermis, which cut me up not into imaginable, traditional pieces (trunk, limbs, head, various organs, skeleton), but into millions of parcels of flesh, forcing me to imagine my final disintegration. An ant doesn't contain you, it can't devour you whole. It requires millions of ants. The fly was diurnal, active, unique, respectable, and even a bit pretty; it was really part of (. . .) everyday life, it was one of the anonymous signs of the cycle of seasons. It is true that by refusing to spit it out, and by commenting on it in nonquotidian circumstances, rather, nocturnal circumstances because of what gave rise to them, I chose to admit the material existence of my body without giving the fly the privilege of intervening—and it would certainly have been invasive, swarming, burdensome.

But: victory of existence, of the concrete, of the most everyday. The I-am-here of the fly had taken that divine, prophetic breath out of me, that breath fired up by numbers, scarcely an hour after my decision to wordlessly do away with, down to the last trace, that singular, ephemeral being. The relation fly/Coca-Cola, in its banality, was not without analogy to the imposing symmetry of the relation life/tres-pass. It was in me that the absurd separation of genres and of styles had taken place. Luckily, there was this plowed, seeded Paris, there was the story of 533-33-13, there's T.t.'s smile here and there, an everyday thing, it reminds me that what comes our way, whatever its origin and its apparent value, is a good thing for us. He saw the gnat beat its wings, then he saw it disappear into my mouth, and gently, patiently, he waited for some vital sign of the gnat to appear, one day or never. For everything that exits, including ants and flies, numbers and words, interests us.

That's what I told L., emphasizing especially the delicate constancy of our being-together: luminous knowledge of everything that happens, through us, to us, from the smallest to the most immense, etc.

★

It was Jensen's *Gradiva* that she had brought me, in that out-of-print edition that bears the touching marks of the circumstances of its printing, the haste and absentmindedness, brought about by the war, which generated a certain blurriness and a substantial number of errata they had indicated, on top of which were several errors that went unnoticed. It appeared to me that, until that evening, when I came to know the text, I had never questioned the name that became the title: "la Gradiva"; I had never read it, I had never as yet heard people tell about it. And I had waited to read it, not knowing if I was waiting to read it (the book, itself read by Freud) or to read her (to find her, but who?).

I wanted to read the *Gradiva* all at once, at night, in bed; I promised myself a short, intense pleasure.

I didn't really care, I could have done without it, I hadn't sought it out.

It was someone other than myself who had been spoken about.

My reading was not without a motive beyond the book: I would find distraction in the morsels of time that separated us. I would sap my impatience. I would temper my unused force in T.t.'s absence.

I would be someplace I am not. What does he do when he is not here?

I do la Gradiva. Iva. I.va. That word is hateful. Making an ignoble, obscene, imperative verb out of it: let's gradivate, Avidarg, it's noon the hour of the *gras* [fat]. Let's do the Avid Rag, Rad I Vag, it's midnight the hour of the Diva.

★

Luckily, he hasn't read the *Gradiva*. Are you happy? Yes. Are you happy? Yes, oh yes. A word that ordinarily puts me in raptures, a synonym of its subject, he is Happy. Who is he? Happy. Who is it? It's Happy, he who says he is.

Norbert Hanold (Old lecher) asks the girl if she would lie down on the ancient paving stones, in the longwise, abandoned, mortal position that she was in when he followed her in a dream as far as this place where she was stretched out calmly, with the same inscrutable sureness as when she was walking *festina lente,* so that death would take her gently and keep her forever after.

She does not say no. She disappears.

Norbert Hanold asks the girl to lie down for him, he even goes so far as to beg, with a visionary ardor, for if the girl were to repeat the dream scene, he would recognize it, he would be

14

sure that it was really her that death had taken before his very eyes, without protest or struggle; thus if the girl were willing to give in to death, he could believe his eyes, she wouldn't need to die really, for she would have only to imitate the mortal position for him to be sure of seeing the girl he had already seen; and if the folds of her dress drape down as the folds of the other one's dress, then their bodies are the same, and he has contemplated the other one so well that each fold is engraved in his memory, for he has the trained eye of the archaeologist who knows stone chips and dust particles and the secret curves of inscriptions; were he to check it out by a hundred concrete proofs that she is indeed the one who had given herself up to mortality, that would prove that, he would be so Happy, would you do me the honor, the joy, the favor of lying down here, of turning your back to me, your legs scarcely bent, your head tilted forward (for that which is remembered in the memory is from the past, is repetition directed toward the past, whereas repetition strictly speaking is a phenomenon of memory directed toward the future)— but he remembers her in the future, Miss could you die and then come back, then later if you please, die and come back again, etc. . . . . I would be so Happy.

She does not say no, she disappears in the present somehow or other and without lying down or dying.

★

We walk a narrow path. At times the path is reduced to an abstract itinerary detached from the earth and suspended, far off, out of sight, in a vaporous network above abysses, chasms, where I know someone is walking, perhaps I, here, but I'm far from the summit, I'm still on this forestage, no less steep and without any real horizon, for the one I see in the distance is an illusion. Only the immediate is real, a narrow spiraling path along the side of a mountain, broad but not high, comic hence mythic. He is in front, I behind him, while somewhere down below I have to sneak in, Vincenneding toward the wings [*hors de vinscène*],* through narrow slots in a grating that is cut without foundation and whose sharp-pointed profile (glass, steel) will scratch me, cut me. When I protest and say it's enough (to die from), someone behind me cuts me off and says instead: it's enough to tear your clothes on.

Behind him, whose back I see, gradual ascent. She is the front, he is the back of a being seen by her and composed of an inconceivable back with front, a being gaping with its outer face, closed off, muddled along its inner walls. She desires his front. She has his back.

★

Saturdaysunday coupled back to back, sides ripped open, mash of hours, flayed beast, without night skin, a bloody raw time, red gut shot through with jolts, monstrous tussle that lays out on my bed its destructive couplings of which I am the disgusted witness, the actor enraged with a culminating force, the rejected, beaten, mangled spectator, at times rejected from the violent bed, at times ejected to be back there and put on the chopping block, excoriated, dreamed of till the end of the gut that chops, at which point I come out calling for the end of the dream, a call that is heard by the dream and that starts it up again, and while I accuse the dream of being an imposter,

*It is important to note in the portmanteau word *vinscène* a pun on *Vincennes,* a Paris district and the location of the University of Paris-VIII from 1968 to 1978, the new campus demanded by and granted to Cixous and other radical professors following the events of May 1968. *Hors de vinscène* is a neologism built on *hors scène,* meaning offstage.—TRANS.

a simulator, a backslider, my accusation is dreamed of as accused, pushes me into the red mouth which sinks its fangs into my throat; I disentangle myself by strangling the mouth with great effort and with a hand full of blood I search, I touch, I turn on the light. He says to me at once: "Turn it off. I want to see the night." He gives me an order. I turn off the light and tell him my dream in a low voice, but I don't know which day it is and I think back to days past on the chopping block. Paris is far. T.t. is far. Paris is misty. The last time I saw T.t. he smiled. Everything was in order. And it is now in this instant and for the first time that I learn, as if I'd heard it from someone, of our separation. In my dream, which one, I had forgotten the infinite lengths of time that had gone by, I had gone back without realizing to the earlier time. In a while I shall wake up old with him dead, and in truth I'll be dead too, already dead were I not to dream again. So long as day doesn't break. But which day? There are times when I wonder: just where has existence gone to? Such as now when breathing one more time becomes nearly impossible, when the next inspiration is uncertain, when my collapsed lungs can't remember the taste of air, when I'm going to die in this dream which I feel is dreaming me, and if I wake up, I'll be dead.

The situation is what it is. At times the tables turn and I see the other side, and I can't even imagine anymore what there was two minutes before, and my body is all that remains of that time there was before, just two profound minutes ago. There also remain: the bed, the room, the lamp, the bedcovers, the clothes, several hundred proofs, and clues both hot and cold, ashes of his cigarettes. The *Gradiva* remains. It's a fantastic tale written in minute detail that pins the sphinx to the real world with thousands of (almost) invisible little stitches. The hero is a savant. He is fairly young and seductive.

For me the ordinary is extraordinary. For him the extraordinary and the ordinary get mixed up, that's why he doesn't see that all things and all events and all women have two sides, which are the ordinary and the extraordinary, the feminine and the masculine, Saturday and Sunday, night and day; because he is a savant. And especially life and death, according to whether you turn your eyes toward yourself or toward the other.

Saturday morning, a joy greater than myself. Saturday night, however, darkness. The same Saturday but turning, veering, fabulizing itself.

★

The *Gradiva* can be read bit by bit, provided that the overall order is respected. I was waking up I was falling asleep, in between I was reading, then I slept while reading and I woke up; I was reading, I read everything I was sleeping I was rereading. All of that reiterated, reading, waking, sleeping, reading, waking, and in the end in an order that was no longer exactly that of the reader seated in daylight, in reading position down to the vertebra, and with one's body arranged first with a view toward action. I was reading and my body followed, we walked one behind the other along the narrow, nameless edge that has neither aim nor necessity, and which flows between one (masculine, indefinite unique, chosen, singular, unknowable) and the other (masculine-feminine-neuter, dependent, attractive, disturbing, desirable), between that which is without any doubt day and that which is without any doubt non-day. I became exhausted. What's prowling around?

★

The bed had become hard, I put up with it. Later I was lying on my side, at the height of night, and I was the one cutting into it, mangling it, pulverizing it by crushing it between my bones and the bed frame. Each time one of us, the night or I, gained upon the other, the bed calmed down, I saw it bend back, relax, smooth out its convulsions as if I weren't there. Meanwhile, I read. At no time, even in the darkest moment, was the thread of meaning broken: I picked up the *Gradiva* at the word where I must have left off to beat off an attack. But I was overcome by the anguish of the duration, I had become a slip beaten by the red sea and at times I felt a desire for the breach, to open up, to move up, to sleep up. I was worn thin, I was dulled down.

★

One day not long ago, crouching down in a sunlit garden, I again saw an earthworm: once in the garden, when I had the right of childhood, I had watched—without counting the displacements, the condensations, the stretchings, the replacements, the avoidances—ants, worms, flies. Especially ants and worms, whose importance I did not underestimate. Worms are blind muscles and seem endowed with a nervous system susceptible to very violent shocks: they expend an extraordinary propulsive energy to move through space, contracting their thin pink casing from ring α to ring ω; imagine if to crawl or to climb or to lie down we had to charge our whole body down to the tips of our fingernails, if our legs carried only themselves and all our organs had to be motorized. We would be a body in disequilibrium then that would project us in every direction according to which system prevailed over which. The worm pushes itself forward, the head strikes out to the left, the tail twists to the right, and the movement continues for itself, for the worm goes nowhere. Sometimes it encounters the other, often an ant. I could never figure out if the ant bites the worm, if it kisses it, if it carries it. It touches it. The worm drawing back doubles up with a start, then takes a desperate leap, with such force that it flies over itself. Pain wrests it away from its own nature, it comes to know the soft hollows of the air. Its flight is a cry, I've heard it. It is not known thereafter what becomes of it.

★

I was bitten by a mouth so small, so alien, so black that, despite the pressure that riveted me to the bed, a spasm lifted me, my arms back in force came round me, restored appearances for me, fixed up the unmade bed on which I was sitting to finish my reading. At last I was now thinking only of what I was reading. I was struck by the luminousness of the narrative, by its intrepid flow, by N.H.'s search as he found time and space unhesitatingly, by the insubstantiality of the vegetable or animal realms, false flowers false lizards: under this huge sun there were no colors; what was seen was a negative, light hadn't broken through the world except at a few minuscule points: a yellow neckerchief, a red rose, a green clasp.

★

I hadn't forgotten the green envelope riddled with hieroglyphs into which my friend M. had slipped a testamentary letter for me. I read it, not without some repugnance caused by the very form of the signs that had scratched, furrowed the soft bosom of this paper.

But I hadn't answered, because it was impossible to answer without killing M.; the way they say that you shouldn't call out to a sleepwalker by name. If I had moved, he would have moved after having destroyed all the space around him. And if I didn't answer, if I let him figure out my silence, there would be a chance—the one there always is, the last, the unknown—that he would come up with an answer himself. This is not satisfactory. That's why he wrote me the other letter, but this one was written in his voice: it was short, he reproached me for having led him up to the gates of the town and not helped him enter. Town was to be read as in the Bible, and I recognized one of those obsessive acts that M. is given to, which consisted in showing me how rich his words were in meaning, rich and full, and how he treated women, whom he always called Girls. I had left him at the gates of the Town [*Ville*]—Girl [*Fille*]—Life [*Vie*]–Vile [*Vile*]. How could the clear sonority of this reproach escape me?

He was standing before an ancient gate, in stone, very high, higher than all the town gates, of a height exaggerated even more by the obliqueness of the wall in relation to the horizon. For this gate was a gigantic wall, whose top he doubtless didn't see because he was at the foot of the gate, but which I perceived as inhumanly high because I wasn't as close to it. A temple wall. I didn't close off the temple to him, nor did I close the gate in the wall. But if it was clear that this immensity was a temple wall, there was not, and never had been, any temple; there was only this wall, and behind it, nothing. What kept the temple waiting was the perfection of the wall. "You have refused me access to the town." I didn't answer. I didn't turn away, so I could hear. The blame brought about a haziness in me, but it was slight. I had refused, but there was no reason. He didn't have an ear into which I could have given him an answer. I knew the nature of his distress, the horror of the non-place, extremity, that corridor between the desired being and the realization that being doesn't exist, between the end of life and death, intolerable corridor, without walls, without presence, overwhelming, invisible, where immortality lies dying. One word too many and I'd kill him. I led him to believe that he could have lived. I was not unaware of the imperfection of my silence. Because of all that, or more precisely because there was such suffering around me, I was veiled in mourning: I felt the somewhat aggravating softness of a fabric of animal origin, a silk no doubt like a transparent gray shantung, a little veil sometimes stiffened into a visor. I entered with sadness. I woke up. I woke up poorly: it was like a missed entrance, a miscalculated leap, a compromise that did me violence. A part of me had not followed, but which part? In a stupor, weary, I missed jumping into bed and scratched my nose, between my eyes, I don't know how. There are areas of very thin flesh with very good circulation: this bit of cut skin discharged an amazing quantity of blood. Blood makes a spectacle that ordinarily amuses me. Something was running down my face and all the tricklings of my existence were r/ejected into it, all the tears and the losses, and the outpourings of energy, of joy, of trust, all the hemorrhages and bleedings, right in the middle of my face.

There is no blood in the *Gradiva*.

★

If your only virgin daughter had betrayed you, you couldn't move a finger without another wound opening in your flesh from whence she sprang. You couldn't turn your face toward a doubtful god, doubt would be your god, your bread, your sun, your time. You would no longer dare walk, for your legs would have betrayed you. You wouldn't be able to stay up or to sleep. How can you trust the earth when your flesh has run away? How is it credible that this flesh is your flesh when the flower of my body poisons my breath? How can I live when the life of my life is my death? If the only daughter is pregnant, then the palace caves in around the builder, the rock turns back into flesh. It is even possible that you envy the heavy, imperceptible waiting for the red infant that you see through the wall of your transparent, your only daughter's belly. For outside, the walls of the houses crumble and spread their mass into the streets. And life holds faster to him than he does to death. Now, can the father be the son? And if your mouth is full of ashes, how can your soul cry out? And if catastrophe had struck on a Sunday, wouldn't that Sunday be in another state of time than the Saturday when you were still a virgin, and wouldn't Saturday have been lived by someone else, whom you envied? Nevertheless, you'd dare to believe that "this can't go on for long," that no matter how great the outrage might be, there's a limit to everything human, and that no matter how choked up you are, in the end you'd burst through it—in the end.

★

At the end of the night, there was no day. I said that I had awakened as one misses a step, I was at the threshold, lying down and yet standing on the edge of Sunday, exhausted, weighed down by the ruins of the night, and even by Saturday's revels. I couldn't have been more beaten down than if M.'s wall had tumbled down onto my back while I was sleeping. I felt no desire [*envie*]. I wasn't alive [*en vie*]. It was the same thing: a heavy abyss, a nervous pregnancy, a desire turned back. The murderous weight of nothingness. An unmovable body, its bones screwed onto the specific structure, its flesh overtop, painted, still. And inside, a fearsome, volcanic reservoir of doubt. Had I taken care to hear his last words? He had said to me: I am Happy. Yes. But these words were not the last. Was something in me supposed to flee? He had said three things, one, two, and three, but maybe the third was the first, and the second the third, etc. Ordinarily, I hold on tight to his last word, which I then link up to the first word he'll say, thus never interrupting our talk, which keeps on reseeding its field, to the point of preventing today a future meaning. In my joy of Saturday I had skipped this love rite. But the word was lodged in one of the three last things, which I proffer here out of order; he said: if I were to die, your breath could bring me back from the dead. And I believed him. Just before or just after, he said: can you, in me, be everything that you want to be? And I said: yes. Yes, when you're here. He spoke to me then (just before or after), concisely, about the room to which he would withdraw, naked, to think, and from which, in the distance, he'd sometimes talk to me.

He had said: Nothing can happen to us.

And I had said: Everything will happen to us. And it was the same thing, at least I thought so, it was that thing, love, with its symmetrical faces and its crooked smiles. Between us there was all this Nothing of Everything, this possibility of the impossible that happened, that would happen at one time or another, here or there (which had become homonyms, and I answered to *where are you?* at times with *I am here,* at times with *I am there,* and it was the same place, for the place where he is I am, the place where I am he is in flesh and bones and the spirit of him or me). But today, here, where are my flesh and bones? I want to arrive, but I don't have a body in which to make an appearance.

He is here, in this room.

I listen. He explains to me how he sees me here. Where I am not. I listen. I don't want to know. It's his business. That. That's none of my business, but he says that in this r   he's watching me. I'm watching myself here.

That's why I love the *Gradiva*: it doesn't want to be looked at in a place where it is not. That's not sufficient reason to love it, and I don't really love it. There's something else.

I quash that gaze, I flatten those eyes that knock you over. I am hurled down, I'm not the one doing the hurling.

I can, in you, be everything that I want to be (but where is that which I want?) on condition that I can be where you are. When you are in this room, where am I? In you who are in her in whom I cannot be? I am shattered. I am devoid no doubt of the membranes of Wisdom and Equanimity. But if I were on guard, if I stood up for myself, I would betray him, I'd be pregnant. Isn't he the one in whom I must be me?

L. says that the reason I don't stand up for myself is that I have a certain aptitude for creative betrayal.

He also said to me: "You're hard on me." Not last Saturday, the one before. I remember clearly. That Saturday I couldn't make up my mind to disappear, I couldn't take my eyes off his drawn features. Who could assure me that I would see him again? Even before the moment of disappearance, he had stopped doing it to me. The day was torn apart, unrecognizable, in places ground to dust. "I'm not feeling well. I'm tired." His fatigue: my own; I severely took him to task for his mortality. How could we be purified? He had cast everywhere the shadows of the end. "Why don't you do it to me anymore? Why have I got to get *myself* up?"

"You're hard on me!"

"But I'm a thousand times harder on myself, because touching you is the same as touching myself."

★

I go out into this narrow garden bordered with high walls through which I must pass in order to reach the little door in the back, on the right, which opens onto this street, back there where I can't see, I go out into Broad Daylight, Bright as noon, everything is too luminous, I come from the background, that is, from the front of the scene, into this intense garden, I come as a voyeur.

★

There is a faceless man with me. At that moment my father's eldest sister comes toward me from outside. The energy of her pace I find surprising. I can explain this: "My aunt walks toward me with the energy and vitality characteristic not of her but of my mother." She wants to take us away with her, the man and me. I sense that it's T.t., but it's not very clear. She brings us two bouquets of flowers. The flowers are a brilliant white, abundant, and particularly fragrant. They are bouquets of lily of the valley. I'm surprised because I hadn't realized it is undoubtedly the month of May. I can hardly believe it, actually. That, too, I can explain: "My father's eldest sister rolled out flour, the last family Sunday, and promised to make me those rich, round cookies that I liked only because she had made them, sweet heavy cookies that I eat with a symbolic enjoyment. In her minuscule kitchen, oven-baking enough chickens for the whole family gathered round the table, on that last Sunday, my aunt sobs, hiding her tears behind her kneading action: 'What love you have for your father! Didn't know anybody could be loved like that.'" My father's eldest sister has a large bosom that I liked to use back then for sleeping against. My father was born in May, a sacred month.

My father's second sister is very very thin, practically a skeleton. This woman with the big heart venerates my father and carries on with him a fantastic incestuous relationship. She has never had children, but she squeezes me and consumes me. Mmm, mmm! Is that good! Say, mind if I eat you up, little girl? She bribes me by acting as medium and message-bearer from my dead father: "If you believe in dreams, then look, you probably saw your father two nights ago, that was him, it's almost as though I'd seen him myself." This industrious woman was named Deborah, which she said means "bee" in Hebrew.

Charmed by the flowers, I rejoice in my aunt's gesture. I bring the bouquet to my face to intoxicate myself with its fragrance. With an incredible violence, several bees dart out of it and swoop down on me, aggressive missiles, landing in twos and threes on my mouth, with a few going for my ears and my throat. They're fat and their buzz is loud. I'm scared. I swat at them with my arms, which only increases their relentless activity. They regroup and charge again. I show them to Deborah, who is standing to my right and whom I feel press against my side. I'm really scared they're going to sting me, they could cut off my breathing, I'd die. Deborah cautions not to move at all, they'll calm down and fly away. One bee crawls along my lower lip: I follow Deborah's advice and shut the terror up inside me, but this results in an intolerable stiffening; my neck becomes a burning column, my body will never be the same. It seems to me as though to escape death I have to play dead. Which way to turn? It's already impossible to move. Shall I talk to T.t. about the emissaries of May, about how these flowers of life secrete death, about my dead father's aggression? Something holds me back, like a fear of revealing to the enemy my weak point where he can kill me. I remember the fatal phrase: "I shall die the day that I can no longer make love with you." Ever since, I'm always on the lookout for that day. Because of my dread of it, I invoke it; making love [*faire l'amour*] becomes a little more, each day, making death [*faire la mort*]; T.t. cannot bring my father back to life, T.t. is mortal; if we never made love we would never make death; I accuse him of dissimulating the traces of his mortality; does he know I can't forgive him his insomnia, his fatigue, his tension, he stabs me with fear at every instant, I accuse him of murder, I reproach him in anguish and with pity for not being God. He promised me to resuscitate if he were to die. My dead father cannot die anymore. T.t. can do anything. He can kill fear, but he's got to kill each fear, the next one, then the next, and on and on. Can he bring my father back to life?

The archaeologist is interested only in what no longer is; he offers the Gradiva a branch of asphodels. These flowers are white as wax and the Gradiva likes only flowers red as blood. The pained fear I feel again when T.t. fails to conceal his mortality is covered by resentment. When I strip it bare, it is infinitely mild; I forgive him, I feel the old gnarled hand of remorse clutch me by the throat; all these feelings seem to me strangely ancient, displaced, excessive, disproportionate to their cause, therefore ridiculous and obscure. They emerge from an antiquated and forgotten region without my being able to take a stand against this extravagance.

★

The dress that the Gradiva wore the day of the eruption covered her down to her ankles, but the large number of folds that gave it body below the waist made what might have been a heavy skirt that interfered with her walking an extraordinarily supple garment. For shoes she had on sandals. The springiness of her step was due also to an ordinance about the way paving stones were to be laid in these towns, wide enough and spaced far enough apart that they get children used to and give them a taste for a bouncing gait. Under the pleated fullness of her skirt, the girl gaily bent her knee, took pleasure in feeling her muscles tense up in the dream of a run she would never make now in broad daylight, but which she could be caught at in the solitude of dawn. The folds of her dress allowed for this dance that couldn't be seen, except by the trained eye of a savant, and revealed what was excessive and beautiful in the position of the second foot, which she drew up nearly vertically toes to heel. I knew that position well, I do it myself. T.t., too, walks flexing his walking muscles. This way we have of imitating elevation, flight, doesn't fool anybody: those who use it spot one another right away; they know, by the verticality of the foot, in which direction, toward which happy space of strength, you are headed. This is why Norbert Hanold spent days looking in vain at the women's legs as they lifted up from the ground onto their tiptoes, effortlessly going through their everyday paces, yet never finding an equivalent for the winged ease of the Gradiva. Most women are slow and languid; a few go faster, but they are unaware of the mysteries of verticality.

★

With her right hand the Gradiva lifted a flap in her skirt of many folds to facilitate her footing. But she could have moved around without this opening in the folds, which would have hidden the movement without preventing her from moving forward. These folds, because of their number and their flow, echoed the freedom of the foot, reverberated with her quick movement down to the last undulation, could conceal under their graceful ruffling the forms of life, thus assuring the secret life of that woman whose charm remains a mystery to this day.

★

What does one think of when one is taken violently by surprise by a breaking loose of Nature, and when the earth plunges into its own abysses, under the feet of the survivors? It is personally difficult for me to respond to this question, but I can give two different answers, in appearance incoherent or contradictory, and in whose folds life got the better of death: a relative, cousin to my father and mother of a large family, was caught in the fracas of an earthquake that swallowed up several thousand of her neighbors and demolished two-thirds of the little town she escaped from in the middle of the night, without even bothering (she confessed this to me later) to count the children, reckoning with a quick glance that they were all bound to be there—that glance got them through to the future, already; while her house was caving in, she was planning its reconstruction, and even figuring how much time it would take. Busied with calculation, she scrambled over a wall sticking up like the prow of a ship toward the sky and got as far as the armoire that had somehow managed during this terrifying night to become lodged upright, fixed, as though turned back into a tree. My relative took out of it her two jewelry boxes in which she had stockpiled, as was the custom in that country, a good part of her fortune. The troop in nightshirts, led by the one who carried their minted future in those chests, arrived at our door, in the neighboring town, just at the moment we were learning of the incredible event. Most of the children were speechless. I was the one who opened the door. I wasn't thinking anything at the time, so entirely impelled was I toward those who had escaped death; I was devoid of any emotion save that of stupefaction. Upon seeing me, the constructive mother burst into tears and with force and timidity threw her arms around me. She was very short, so that I found myself carrying her, squeezing her and at the same time being squeezed by her, almost consoling her. I hadn't seen her since my father's death, she told me; and I mused that ten years had gone by and that she must have given birth to about ten children, all of them my cousins, those who were standing in a circle around us. Then she made me accept the largest bracelet from her case, in the night, in a nightgown permeated with that odor of sulfurous dust, mud, and dried blood that the gutted earth exhales.

★

Kleist* tells a vertical story: everything happens very fast, rises, comes to an end, exhibits itself at a very high level, with great strength, and without the slightest consideration for

*Heinrich von Kleist; the story retold here is that of "The Earthquake in Chile." —TRANS.

morality or prejudice, without a link in that invisible network of the Law, which is like the network of blood vessels in our eyes and which subtends all writing, acting as its predetermining phantom, without any possibility that a convention of any type, in any society, might be able to hold it back. This is that writing of the above-and-beyond that resembles the verticality of the Gradiva's right foot: these are beings who know that the future is not a time that comes toward us as we move toward it along a horizontal path, but that it is this high-level present, whose limit we can never know, a mitigated time, whose principal quality is strength. This strength is absolute, divine, free from any human project, implemented totally in the sole divine project, which is to spread life out to its outermost borders, at the risk, run a hundred times, of meeting up with death. It's the story of the earthquake in Chile. Kleist tells how the young Jeronimo, accused of a crime, was standing against a pillar of the prison where he had been confined, and he wanted to hang himself. The prison, the pillar, the hanging, the only daughter, the garden, the feast of Corpus Christi, the Carmelite dress of the many folds, the child who suddenly comes out, during the procession, from among the folds, the young man, the garden, the prison, the pillar. The felicity of omnipotence. The prison of impotence within the prison. The stairs, the steps, the getaways checked by the standing arches, against a pillar, with her lying down on the steps with the child amidst the folds. In the garden already closed on five sides, the sixth wall was aerial, above them, their future, the high-level present. All the masks of the law rush headlong to see how they make out, in the hope that the young man and the girl won't be able to take off. A sixth wall is placed over them; there's a funeral procession for him, at the end of which his head will be cut off, in front of the whole family: sisters, brothers, bishops, laws, and virgins. To get a better view of his head popping off, the virgins pop off the roofs of houses, for they have the future ahead of them to rebuild them.

One page further on, everything is reversed: what was up is down, the sky has fallen to the earth, the sixth wall has crumbled, the other walls have buried the law, the young man who wanted to hang himself from the pillar is clinging to that same pillar so as not to be knocked down. The main prison gate has been broken through from the outside and is so disintegrated that the floors and wall sections form a thousand monstrous wrinkles across the earth heaving in labor. And amidst the debris of God the Mother, from the most holy and unique Virgin, Absolute Justice at last is born, whose always open eye knows no moderation, and which has neither memory, nor virtue, nor scourge, nor measure.

★

He wants to kill himself but he doesn't want to be killed. If he were killed, he would be dead. His death: a rope tied to a pillar in a prison. There's no more prison, and he clings to the pillar.

★

When T.t. calls me I can't help talking to him about the *Gradiva*. Or rather, I can't help talking to him about every other thing and it's the *Gradiva* that keeps breaking in. He hasn't read the book; I ask him what the name of it reminds him of, and he says: of an Italian opera, but he denies that it's because of the similarity with "la Diva." I see a Fat Diva [*Grasse Diva*], he refuses to see that. In exchange I let him in on a discovery: in this volume printed under difficult conditions, during the war, there are a few errors. I shall tell no one, except him, that on two occasions you find *Gravida*.

★

What is an eruption? It can't be held back. I can't help myself. I can't hold it back. Better the rips, the cracks, the collapses, the carved mouths where there are no throats, the entrails showing—better all that than this apparition: that which is projected outside me and covers over me, this body foreign to my body that rises from my body and shrouds it.

★

I could have disappeared into a crack, into a hole of being, and quickly. But I suffocated under an excess of being. I was standing on the edge of Sunday; I wasn't cut off from the world. To be sure, the streets were blocked with rubbish and the ash reached at one point up to my neck, but I could still move, I wasn't in danger of dying, at least my body wasn't. I saw everything, I heard fine, I wasn't hurting. I didn't want anything, I was remembering another time, in another place, but it wasn't a memory that came from then to now and that might have burst into my consciousness. There was a thick ash curtain between me and everything that was going on there. I saw that there was a memory, but the curtain kept it so far away that it could never infiltrate me. It was a distant, insignificant assailant. An anonymous coupling was seen there. It was T.t. and I, or the young man and the girl, or the Gradiva and her Hanold, most probably us actually, but it depended on the memory of where it happened; now, my memory was disconnected from my body, and the only thing that remained clear to me was precisely oblivion. I couldn't transform the memory into something for my good, it didn't fly off, it started all over, but impossible to make it go in: either I was the one who no longer knew which way to move forward and I was standing outside the time I was living, scarcely held in place by this slender cord of memory along which T.t.'s voice would always pass, or else it was the memory that couldn't find my eyes to memory and that remained outside; or else there were my eyes over there, full of memory, and I over here consigned to an ashy dungeon. I was in a state of imperfect disappearance, the kind that's neither fish nor fowl, neither rope nor pillar, neither empty nor full. The ashes were starting to sap my strength, to mop up my blood and my colors, and my vigilance. I trimmed the vestiges of my consciousness down to one bit of knowledge: Sunday is a day of limited free time followed by another day that is off-limits to T.t. So, all I'd have to do was to hold out till the next day by saving my breath. But my desires dried up, my emotions wore out, my muscles slackened: I couldn't hold out anymore for anything. If he had said to me: *hold me, hold me!* my arms would have disobeyed. To hold onto him, so he wouldn't forget me, I tried to seduce him, I told him strange, true stories, such as the one about my imaginary attempt at translation: wishing to translate the German name of the *Gradiva,* because of the ashes that at times weighed down my tongue until I had wetted them enough to swallow, my tongue often forked; at least that's the reason I came up with to explain painlessly my backsliding; it was this explanation I was using when he was taken aback. In truth I was really sad, I shouldn't have said it, or I shouldn't have failed to say it, or I should have refrained from saying it; *Gradiva* is only a pseudonym; it signifies "she who has the luminous, or light, step." The true name of the Gradiva is a German girl's name that it seems to me impossible to preserve in a translation, for the girl's false name is hidden there: the reader must know that the Gradiva and the girl are the same person in two different languages. If I translated this text, there would be a third Gradiva; if I didn't translate the German name, Gradiva would no longer be the girl. I propose to translate this strange and virginal girl's name with its exact French equivalent, which is the compound word *Mortbelle* [Beauteousdeath]. To be sure, the presence of the letter *t* in the middle of this word may appear incongruous to the French eye, but I don't see how it could be suppressed. Is it correct? I hesitate. But then I keep the *t* in. T.t. is surprised to find out that I intend to do a translation, when one exists already, however defective it might be, and when I don't have time to get involved in that kind of work, badly paid besides, and when I've always told him how thoroughly I had rejected any deep investigation into my native language. And what do you think about the *t*? And how was this question left? Norbert Hanold didn't have the courage to pronounce a certain pronoun. To conclude, we agree on this point: it seems to us we've already been talking about all that for some time.

All his talk seems extraordinarily funny to me, because of good faith and deafness. It seems to me that I must have moved tons of rubble et cetera to get back to our initial agreement. It's too gross.

★

In order to rid yourself of a bad dream that's stuck to your body, you have to shake your head very hard. The shaking must be all the more forceful in function of whether it's a dream of a bad dream that would turn out not to be as bad as reality. I shook mine with all my might, and by chance, in the midst of this gesticulation, I found myself suddenly lying down, a bit numb, a bit sad, on my roomy Sunday bed. I was down, a bit numb, a bit sad, on my roomy Sunday bed. I was detached. The sky might have fallen in on my head, I wasn't afraid of anything. I got up. *You're not the one who gets me up when you are not here.*

He is someone I'm talking to myself about. Two thousand years ago I already lived all that, then I forgot it, at least I separated that Life from this life, this Sunday from Saturday. Between the two there was the eruption, which I was unable to hold back, and all my senses changed. The heavy had become light, desire had come under the sway of fear, I no longer needed him, but instead the need to need had surged forth, and this need took up all the space. Nothing was so close to me as this need.

★

The young man had forgotten his desire to die, the name of death, and the cut-off head of death, as the body of death had scared him so much. He touched his forehead and his breast, and he came back to himself. What can one see without eyes? This child who had interrupted the procession when he dropped, all ruddy and headfirst from among the folds, was a boy. One wonders who cut the cord, for the author does not say, but one might think that it was the mother superior in person; what's certain is that the cord was cut, since it is said that the girl was led off to prison, though perhaps it was cut only once she got to prison. Now, while I'm trying to find where to cut in, where to pick up again, she's already nursing. Meanwhile, the mother superior had been crushed, the girl had closed her eyelids. The order of the living had changed: the girl thinks back to the father of her son and waits for him. She weeps, she waits, she bathes the baby, and the author doesn't say if she would have awaited until death the man for whom she had once risked her life.

This is how they spent the night from Sunday to Monday: he had his back against the pilaster of a tree, she was in his arms, with her back against the young man's chest, and the child was in his mother's arms, thus each up against the other, back against heart, and they talked to one another all night about the garden, the prison, the pillar, the rope. The tree was a pomegranate in bloom. A single cloak with broad folds covered all three of them. The ending of this story, which is ancient and unfair, shouldn't be told. I am jealous of that child who stops things up and becomes a burden; my soul, here, is nostalgic for that high-level present no longer practicable.

★

Where are you?

Lying on my side, in the corner of Meleager's garden under my cover of ashes. Waiting. It's been two thousand years since I lay down for you. He'll be surprised when he digs through the ashes to find here no more than my soul, form of forms. As I wait, I become waiting. I am latent. Waiting for you to make me appear. My body was stretched out. Bring me awakening, get me up! I am molded, red clay, originally.

Get me up.

He comes, so I am here. He rouses me, so something stirs in me. He kisses my breast and my belly fires up the channel, the well-pit, the gorge (one of those furrows by which flesh can be traversed by the flow of elements and whose name I do not know, and which link together the most distant points of the body) that plunges from my groin to my knee at first and then into my back, goes along coils of muscles and runs right up to my neck.

But today: inertia. Over there, there's feeling, there's wanting. But here: cutting off, choking up of all the channels, the gorges, the corridors. Impossible in this state to lunge toward anybody. One day I shall take up with myself again. I am in a state of analogy with death in its slowness. *Lente festinans.* "For that's where our tragic aspect lies, that we quit so softly the world of the living, in a simple box." This sentence also is mutilated: I don't know from which text it came back to me and I'm not trying to find out, for it is foreign to me in terms of each one of its words, except for the softness of the departure. Now it awakens in me a concern about departing.

Am I accused of being unfaithful? The flesh of the infidel is a conglomeration of dust, ash, and little stones.

There is no accusation; infidelity is not a transgression; I'm not the one who wanted the eruption along with the ashes and my extinction. There was this time fracture, pumping away, this void sucking to the maximum, this abandoned belly. If I am unfaithful it is because I make his absence manifest. If I am empty, it is because of faithfulness, for I represent his absence.

We forget the dead, then we forget we've forgotten. I do not forget anything. But he's the one who has our living memory, and I'm the one who has the trace. Here, oblivion that remembers. Over there, full, round, plentiful time of our past that will return. Over there, death of time, death of death.

So long as he's not here I have no one to place myself in.

That's why I say this: I am dead. And yet no one has killed me. And it is I who say: I am dead, therefore it is impossible for me to really be dead. But I say: "I feel I am dead," because "I do not feel that I'm living." There's no one where I can live. I have a deep need of your body in order to be.

This room where he is confines me to here.

★

The reason for which the end of the Earthquake must not be recounted is perhaps the following: beginning with the day that follows the day of all the upheavals, and the night when all three are wrapped up alive in the folds of a single cloak which is the young man's, everything falls down and falls away—the vertical present indicates the possibility of the passage from the human to the divine. The divine is that which is outside-the-law, outside all the laws of physics, of morality, of collective prohibition. Until that new day, the young man and young mother's desire is maintained at that level of tension that is higher than life, therefore higher than death. His face turned toward the image of her, he has looked for her through the rubble, with his eyes; her eyes turned toward the memory of that cherished soul that she thought had flown off, the girl had waited a long time for him to appear. During that time their eyes held death off at a distance, and they desired as gods, against death. Their whole consciousness was made from the body of the other, and that body was imperishable. So long as the desired body filled up the world, they could not die, they could not close their eyes, they could not see what was mortal and what was real. There was the broken world, which cried out as it collapsed; there were their bodies, intact and virgin, which called to one another.

The night of the pomegranate tree in bloom they all three go under the same cloak, and they tell each other their story; at the intersection of the two narratives, the child is born. He knows his mother. He twists in the water of the river, he stretches his body between the water and the air, but she holds the little salmon tight by his head. It's the first time that there's water in this tale: up to here, fire, wall panels, holes, ashes, pillars. And especially bodies: bodies to hang, bodies to kiss, bodies to cut up, head separated from body, neck against pillar, neck cut, bodies living in a simple prison, a lost body, a nude cut to pieces. And the imagining: each person wants the whole body of the other in which there is everything.

★

Norbert Hanold fell in love at first sight with the image of a woman walking. The body, depicted at about a third its actual size, had attracted him with such violence that he felt absorbed by this porous figure, into which he was surprised he wished to penetrate as if seeking in some nonexistent depth the mystery of its surface; the porousness itself, which did not open onto any organ, fascinated him by its substantive contradiction. It was open, but nothing came out, nothing went in. Norbert Hanold imagined that he was disintegrating into millions of specks of dust that entered the fresh pores of the figure, but this reverie stirred him without satisfying him. The Gradiva seduced him especially with her smallness and with her immobility and with the inherent contradiction between these two qualities: the smallness of the figure could not take away the impression of height that she made on the eye; the Gradiva had a svelte yet scaled-down body. Norbert Hanold murmured "my great big little thing" when he would dust her off. As for the immobility of her existence, which reassured him, calmed him, attracted him, and finally devoured him slowly, it caused bafflement because of the verticality of the right foot. Who walks without moving? Who rises up without falling back down? There was something of common humanity in her, and it was that gracious, firm body, which would have been desirable if it had been shown in actual size, or which would have been ordinary and negligible if the right foot had followed the left foot and placed its sole and heel on the floor. But because the right foot was forever raised, there was something divine and never-ending about her—not common—which didn't move, which maintained divine immobility. It looked as though the artist had blocked out a clay model in the street, sidestepping life itself. The model, the clay, the sideshow. If Norbert Hanold had been told that what absorbed him was in truth the body of a large woman in motion, would he have believed it? The model is next to life, which is next to the clay. And the body is next to the soul; the shadow is next to the body; the street is next to the garden.

★

In the garden there had been something divine in them: they were not afraid of their mortality, they were impenetrable, and the law twisted its rings and flexed its little round muscles in an attempt to tear itself away from its condition of earthworm. Their immortality had no name, but it fluttered

from one to the other. And there came to them in this unin-
terruptedness a third body.

Now, under the fruit tree in bloom they spoke a great deal,
and their talk ticked off the hours of the night. By dint of talking and listening, stopping at times to kiss the child, they
came to be stunned at still being alive; they started to forgive
others, then to understand, then to pray, to be thankful, to
give, to reunite, to fall, to put the garden behind them. To
embrace their dividedness. This is why the end of the story is
unfair for us who have forgotten mortality, common humanity, and the worm of the law. As a result of their astonishment
at still being there and of the awe with which they looked at
their child, and of thinking of the time when Nature
destroyed everybody but them, they had the extraordinary
impression of being reborn, it was a soul sensation, they
could describe it. A new life drew them forward, unham-
pered, with its streets where they could walk with their heads
high, with its mortal end, where there was no trace left of the
marvelous earthquake.

★

Originally my land was red, the land where I'm from.
When my father died, some time ago, I discovered that he
would change color with time: his land would turn red.
Sometimes I remember him from before his death. He would
wash and get dressed in front of me, and I can see that his
thin, spry back is covered with white skin just barely spotted
with brown marks. I've always been careful not to take T.t. for
my father. I draw attention to all the differences. If T.t. were
dead, he wouldn't have the same red color. Since all the differences are passed on to me from now on, and since T.t.

molds my flesh with my soul and gets me up, I never know exactly what's going to happen when I do get up. I wonder each time who I'm going to arrive as. What's going to surge forth out of there?

That Sunday, however, I wasn't worried, or curious. I was of no account. Heavy and of no account. Immobile, stretched out, brought down, indifferent, back turned, shrunk to a third of my actual size, untantalized by any question, secretive, cold. I don't care. Desire also was with him in the room, I could have remained lying down for a very long time, between Sunday and Monday: it was my lying down, my form stretched out between the days that constituted the materialized divergence, by which Monday was not a piece of Sunday but another time along which my dreams of the edge passed.

/there's the trail whose invisible end is surely death, but it's the only trail. It plunges toward a proximate horizon. Adults must take the narrow path, a sort of edge or bank, to the right of the trail because it is clear. What it's the edge of is not clear, since the edge itself is invisible, though known, present. What is seen is the way into the trail, and we stand on the verge of it. This trail is bordered by young birch trees with light-colored leaves that form a rather vast archway: this is the way the children go because they fit through this opening. A tunnel of frail leaves, beautiful, different from a treeless border. And I protest: why should I deny myself the trail just because it's down there? I don't need to crawl, down close to the ground. I can go along with my body bent over, my head down, and who cares if the branches brush against my neck? I'm not afraid.

Second dream of the edge.

The house, high up, familial, brings everyone together. Suddenly I remember the children. Fortunately my mother has put them over on the side, otherwise they could have fallen from a terrace with no railing. These children are young, pink, plump, desirable. I had them, they died, they are eighteen months old, perhaps they are me, their life is established and they do not think. In the house owners are springing up everywhere. Down below—and that seems very far—a sort of large sidewalk borders nothing. To my surprise, my grandmother, who fears the edge, leans over at the risk of falling.

Dream of the city of death.

He's refusing me everything, not out of meanness, driven only by an egotism that finds complicity in the person of waitresses at this restaurant where we have stopped. None of this is him. The waitress-mistresses are very attentive. They descend, bent forward, from a stairway to the left of our table (we are seen by me in profile) as if from the wings of a stage. Heavy red tapestries. I want, I ask for, a black-currant ice,* which he refuses because it's not necessary, and yet he's offered cigarettes, and that's necessary. At the same time the soubrette brings over a large rectangular case filled with matchboxes. I keenly desire one of those boxes—they're flat, long, narrow, beautiful; I don't need them, haven't the right to them; but I steal one, and in an attempt to camouflage this theft I crush the box in my hand so it will look used, but it's no use, I've been seen, I return the object. I take out a fairly large, flat, red match that's in the box, because it's pretty. He tells me he doesn't need matches because he has a lighter: he shows me its glowing points, hard little bundles of copper

*Glasse, rather than glace, in the original.—TRANS.

with sharp points that I would never know how to use anyway. On the street we're walking along where there's no more heather, we'll have no more heather. Instead, there are flowers of death: I get a glimpse of an odd little girl with flaxen tresses who has just placed a corn sheaf on the edge of the sidewalk next to others. I figure out that this is a commemorative town. The street at the center is marked by staggered rows of floral crowns: the opposition must have been beaten down in tightly closed ranks. At one end a woman, back turned, places her flowers, then gets up—a satisfied, disburdened look on her face, large glasses, total indifference to death—and she's just taken a poop. Further on we see a sparsely wooded pine grove; these trees are aimed, no doubt, at making up for the heather. But no assurance is kindled in me. I don't deny the need to appear: I know; but it's impossible for it to be said. I know why I'm still dead the night before Monday, even if it's temporary: the need is on the inside, in the lower depths, and it isn't coming back up. It's not my fault. For something strange is happening: for this need to surge up again, the way will first have to be clear, then I'll have to be able to say it. Then, because of my saliva and my muscles, it would be *my* need. But in order to say something a whole apparatus is necessary (larynx, vocal cords, mouth, teeth, tongue, and words). I have everything that's necessary: young, strong, well-trained, the apparatus that says me has never failed. In certain horror stories the hero experiences a shock so great that he loses his speech, his hair turns white overnight, etc. People don't believe it, but these are familiar symptoms. The muteness and whiteness signify white death, a retirement away from life yet on this side of death. But you don't see people in the street whose hair has turned white out of fear. The white remains hidden. There is fundamentally a hidden white need, and above a bed of ashes and on top of that my red land.

Missing from this need to go out and begin is speech. His mouth is my mother, and we speak the same language, the same tongue moves for us both. He's the one down there who's got my tongue. I open my mouth in front of the mirror, and in the dazzle of my white teeth that light up the perfect matrix I don't see my tongue. During the wait, everything is written, fundamentally, out of need. Here's what is written on the tablets of need: Get me up.

Speak me (be word of me so I can speak).
Say me (Say me Myself).
All that is traced in dust, making reading difficult. Then it cries out, it flashes:
Get me out
Go out
Go out
Go out
Get Me out so I can go back in
Open, open.
I want to die away from here, where everything is mute because everything is deaf.

The expression "a dull pain" twirls itself in my ears, deforms and reformulates itself, and finally reveals itself: it involved a heavy softness, or a softness that was heavy. In fact, my heaviness is soft and even flabby. It has the weakness of modeling clay, the false resistance of those metals that can be engraved with no effort. He will have no trouble lifting me up. The Gradiva, because of what she carries in her and what she

wears, was much too heavy for Norbert Hanold's muscles. He's
not the one who lifted her out: not only did she pull herself
out of the trap of time by herself, but also she took Norbert
Hanold by the body, and she transplanted him in the present
of the future, that horizontal present that human couples like
to walk along arm in arm. Before they die, young human couples take a honeymoon: they travel next to each other, in such
a way that they never see one another face to face. In the
course of the trip they become acquirers of memories.

★

There was no way I could sleep anymore, and no reason to
stay up. Between Sunday evening and Monday I spent hours
looking at my knees. Thanks to the leg joint, it is possible to
walk; but I looked at my knees with no objective, no intention, no desire, no movement. I considered the possibility of
bending. It made some sense if I imagined getting up, and
then took a walk with an objective, maybe even a trip. Perhaps
the recollection of a wedding, which would have taken place
and time in my memory, if I'd been the one who'd had it.

It's always the same story: go out in order to come back
in, leave in order to arrive, begin in order to finish, and vice
versa. I had gone out, left, begun, but everything else was in
his power, except the points of my limbs and of my desires,
which limbs and desires were at that time inert. This story has
already been told, I've already lost all that, and I've already
forgotten, and it's the memory of that forgetting that reassures
me. I know it all in advance: the only part that eludes me is
the ending. Looked at from the other side, from the outside,
the ending could be taken for the beginning: this waiting has
already taken up time, has already come to an end.

We also happened to travel, but not on a honeymoon or side by side; we did it with no objective and with no intention other than attaining together a certain height. Traveling in such a way that the distance separating the two points is just small enough and just great enough that their orthogonals never appear parallel.

★

We walked one behind the other, I followed him, and I couldn't see anything but his back, my eyes fixed on his neck, and I forgot that there were things and that there was a horizon.

Walking behind him, I didn't go faster than he, I pursued myself in him at an equal pace and without knowing it. What an active peace!

What if I had suddenly walked faster?

I walked without fearing a thing.

In a while I'll see him, at the end. He'll turn around. I'll recognize him right away. Can one imagine any greater, any darker joy?

To hold back the sun, to enjoy the end of its absence. To shut your eye.

He was in front of me.
I made ready to place my right foot in front of my left foot, which I raised from the heels to the toes when at last he

arrived. My eyes were open and received his smile, which came not from his mouth but from a certain tension in his eyelids. Which made one understand that the mouth is a third eye.

★

He had arrived and I wasn't making it. Somewhere the fifteen-second angle was firm. Someone threw me off track at the last second. Who has already smiled with this mouth? Dull pain of being laid off without compensation. To which other smile in which face does he refer me to? Up to this point I had lost him, but he has arrived, he's speaking to me, my eyes are open, I'm standing up, but the opening is imperceptible, nothing can pass through. I am lost.

★

Since I wasn't saying anything and was weighing down on him, he placed me on the made-up bed. The bed closes around us. T.t. bends over me. In fantastic tales people keep watch with their eyes closed: in fact, they open their eyes on the other side. This arc formed by T.t. over me constructs a place of repose. When he bends over me, I close my eyes just in time to see a word being written inside: "papa." Absurdly misspelled with an s ("paspa"). No, I say to myself. That's a mistake. He's been dead for a good long time. In the street T.t. is often taken for my husband. He could be my father, but

In general, out of mistrust of myself, I am careful not to draw a parallel by which I might perhaps, in spite of myself, slip into some facile confusion. This is why I emphasize so often the differences (looks, age, origin, particular traits, temperament, fate, etc.), as indicated on the table below, which shows clearly that T.t. cannot be the name behind which my father would be hidden. I also emphasize, in another mental diagram, the differences there are between me-as-lover and me-as-daughter. In any case, I don't act like a daughter with T.t. I've had a chance to verify it on several occasions. Not that I don't want T.t. to be my father, but, knowing myself, remembering every day the time quake that shattered my life when my father suddenly disappeared, I don't want to fall into the facileness of a story that would begin on the blessed day that followed the catastrophe. I've already spoken about all that, two thousand years ago, somewhere else, and in a different language. I know well the form and substance of their bodies, and they don't have a single point in common. If I were going to confuse someone with my father, it would more likely be myself.

My father

Age: 38. Large slender body endowed with a natural elegance, black hair, face very similar to mine, weak constitution, bookworm, leisure walker, authoritarian temperament, castigator, taciturn, possessed of dry humor, origin: dividing line between proletariat and petite bourgeoisie, autodidact, artistically inclined, extremely sensitive, confident, liberal. Fate: to die young.

T.t.

Age: 40. Thin, lean, hard body endowed with a natural elegance, white hair, face without the slightest resemblance to ours, Nordic type, solid constitution, active in sports, leader personality, persuasive, indulgent, no sense of humor, extremely sensitive, harboring no illusions about others, history enthusiast, optimistic, unchangeable, never sick ("strong as an ox," says my mother Eve). Fate: to be pursued.

Thus, when I saw the word written, in the silent darkness deep within me, it felt to me like a gross imposture of myself, an attempt at facile recognition, the way a schoolchild who can't find the solution to a problem will throw out numbers haphazardly with one chance in a billion of getting it right. I didn't get it right; but I did feel slightly ashamed, because of my impoliteness toward T.t. The thought of adultery, or of any other betrayal (and I have some that run through me without leaving a trace, or else I bring them on in order to put some situation or emotion to the test), could fill me with guilt: there's nothing to that. I hold nothing back; on the other hand, any allusion to my father awakens the jealous lover of uniqueness; one can never be wary enough of one's father. Inversely, who knows what the figure of my father might smuggle in?

How do you get proof of an imposture? The word was written, in *bold,* rather luminous letters, in the dark depths of my consciousness. Handwritten; therefore the word was written by someone. It doesn't seem to be me, I don't think it's my handwriting, nor is it a disguised handwriting—or else I would have sensed it. Hence, neutral handwriting. I scarcely start thinking about it when dissociations between beings and their names crop up everywhere, dissociations between truth and its voice. It is I who am author of the word written in a neutral hand. The word is not a name, it's a vocative that runs through T.t. and wants to pass itself off as the object of my desire, to which I am firmly opposed. Two, too facile. All I have left to do is to denounce this semblance of subversion. But why was it written in letters? It looks like an anonymous letter or else a message that aims at remaining secret, which I send myself in silence, and which T.t. wouldn't get wind of unless I transmitted it aloud. What had I intended? What do I want? Everything that is written in the dark depths is part of us. Last remark: the word wrote itself; now, when I think of T.t. I never write it down; I see him, I touch him, I speak to him loud or softly, and I'm the one doing all that, without any intermediary.

I pity my father who is defenseless and who no longer exists. That is absurd.

One more question, just in case: do I want to kill T.t., or do I want him to go find my father and bring him back to daylight? Do I want to see my father again? Absolutely honest answer: I don't want to here and now.

My father and I didn't know each other.

★

Here I stop turning round in circles, and I let the past forage through my entrails. My memory is here, along with my tongue, and there are words coming out of my mouth.

"It's good that you're coming."

As the sun is extraordinarily hot that Monday, to the point of seeming to us to have the ardor of a prediction, our bed catches on fire without burning up; the humming air has a thickness, a strong party smell, and we blithely discuss its nature; I maintain that it's a fresh sea smell, that of the waters of the south whose coming and going through the crevices of the rocks in A. represents for me a primordial rhythm. This rhythm is the heart of an overall landscape that touches and releases each one of the senses and opens all the directions of time and the gorges of consciousness. It smells of the fresh sea, with no dead fish, no rotting algae, the sea in motion, corrosive, singing, hard-hitting, rocking the ancient dead who buried their bones on the edge of the land, on the edge of the sea. A. is the memory of a palimpsest. Peoples have succeeded peoples there, gods have dethroned gods, the dead of one race have kept an eye on the living members of the conquering race, the paving stones have been trodden over the centuries by foreigners, lords, slaves, and no one today remembers, except the skin of the land scarred with minute marks, and all the bones have mingled together. The earth is red and gives way to anyone who wants to dig into it. Death is what happened to my father.

T.t. holds that the smell of the air is that which I introduced him to and which I don't know. Are we thinking of the future? We must hold onto this day of fructification so we can come back to it: this day is a Monday, which will end (or will not end), another day perhaps very remote in time from today.

To us time happens: time is happening to us at all times and even from every direction.

This explains the phrase I said so naturally a moment ago, that I had the impression my tongue was an ear that was listening to itself, is palpitating still, new and mysterious. I feel better since I heard it. The backs aren't turned anymore, I'm stretched out facing T.t., who is bent over me and shades my eyes. He too likes the phrase.

★

When the young Jeronimo was leaning up against the pillar to pass the rope around it, not knowing where the only daughter and the child were, he no longer had time to get a thought in. The author states that his thoughts had wings, but that they bumped against the prison walls. There was neither door, nor light, nor power. Thoughts crashed against the walls and spattered him with blood. The only object that did not reject him was this pillar, to which he spoke softly. The pillar was everything: the girl's body when he put his arms around her, a certain future, presence, proof that he wasn't dreaming, and God. It is possible to say that this column was the form of the time he had left and the end of that time. It's not hard to imagine that the young man experienced for the pillar, and the general separation as well, a sublime love that scorned appearances and wasted no time on vain demands, an imaginary passion so strong that the carved stone yielded to the lips and the ardor of Jeronimo. It is quite probable that as he passed the rope around the girth of the column tears of tenderness blurred his vision, cherished names flowed onto the object's still texture. For it was the only being that was good to him. It is equally probable that when the young man spent the night of his life under the pomegranate tree, he could no longer think about that same pillar without cringing in horror. But this is human. The love he felt for the pillar was divine: it knew no limit, no difference, no memory, no hope, only an omnipotence that was indistinguishable from his life, and from the end of his life. His life, moreover, had no "end" imaginable, since that end could not have been lived and could belong only to the lost, virgin girl. The end was in the column that didn't have eyes to weep for him, ears to hear his last words, arms to hold him, or flesh to shroud him: thus, when Jeronimo kissed the column and called it by his lover's name, he was already dead; his end had no continuation, he had disappeared, his death had no future, no one would tell about it, it would have no past. It had the inconsistency of a present absolutely outside of time. It was dedicated to the absent one, that inhuman, perfect time, without mode and without subject other than the one who was wearing away at the column. In a while he would never have been. He could never return.

Fortunately, the column would remain. Something that he loved would remain. This column was his final hour, his testament, his heir, his child.

★

Long after T.t.'s arrival, I was still sighing over the ineffable well-being resulting from the end of the phrase that he had brought forth and that I heard palpitating, falling, coming back, with an inexplicable sensation of relief. I listened to it, examined it, weighed it, took note of the sequence and of each word as though I were a chemist of the soul, searching for the source of its power. Everything about the phrase pleased me, enchanted me, seemed to me of a much greater density than the simplicity of the words would have led one to expect. It would have been the bearer of only an ordinary meaning if I hadn't perceived in its last word the passionate quaking of conception.

★

After talking all night about the garden and the prison, Jeronimo and the only daughter decided to return to their homeland, where the young man's mother's family dwelled (Spain), in order to live there happily. They were sure that this return to their native ground would be their recompense and their salvation. To get started, they would have to go to the port of La Concepción. The sun was already extraordinarily hot when they stopped talking and fell asleep. Santiago no longer existed, they slept between Chile and Spain without falling, their blood flowed through their bodies, they weren't dead, justice was brought down, the people had a taste of chance; they were walking in a garden of ruins, walls were lying scattered, roofs cracked, palaces smashed, convents gutted, corpses dismembered, heads bashed in, virgins defiled, judgments buried; they passed through the tallest prisons with a steady gait, the tips of their toes scarcely touching the edges of the sunken portals, the only daughter lifted with her left hand a pleated section of her skirt for fear of treading with an ill-informed foot on her father's remains. If the streets are ripped up, where will the procession pass by? If the body of the Law is in pieces, how can its letter be enacted? If the temple is smashed, how will the gods make their way to the lower region? If there's no more door, there's no more passing through. They wanted Spain, they would get there through La Concepción, across the sea, through the gate of Cádiz. Once well inland, they would stretch out a cloak; they would never yet have made love, for in that new world back there the girl was still an only child and a virgin. As soon as the quakes would have stopped. They jumped over the temple pillars, believing that the destruction of things contained the overturning of the Law. As if the soul were the structure of the body. The only thing left standing on the site was a religious building.

★

When he found out the Gradiva's true German name, N. Hanold stared at the slender woman whose gait and the form of whose foot he knew so well; and the tranquil indifference of this smallish face attracted him violently in that this face didn't try to take hold or even to attract. One might have thought it one of those highly wrought, dense writings, or else one of those excavations that had taken up his time so completely that he felt he'd been thrown into it rather than having wanted to go in, and where he could never tell clearly if it was his own project that kept leading him forward or if the exaltation that drove him weren't in fact the inverse of an irresistible attraction exercised by the site of the dig, not because of what he could expect to find there, but in order to plunge into it, abandon himself to it, be preceded by what he'd say about it later in a scholarly paper whose author would be not him but the digs. This obscure feeling of having only to reproduce what in any case awaited him he experienced before the tranquil face that tempted him by not tempting him: by force rather than by judgment, precisely because Hanold wasn't looking to understand but to maintain the surface inviolate, that terrifying virginity of gaze that alighted on the world with the same verticality, sure of itself and ready for flight, that characterized the movement of her foot. Because everything in her was a sign of detachment, he felt the desire for some perpetuity: so he proposes that they take a honeymoon trip to Pompeii. In other words: would you please share this layer of dust with me? Something told him that the sun and the dust were supposed to favor conception by exciting the imagining of the future. The idea of recognizing the Gradiva among the prints filled him with a delicious seriousness.

The proof that this whole story is an invention is in the

return from the Pompeii honeymoon, normal in the case of the archaeologist, but inconceivable for the German zoologist's daughter. This narrative comes to an end like a fairy tale, no doubt because the author wishes to show that his hero is saved, and therefore is no longer afraid of dying, but rather enjoys the spectacle of death which he thought belonged only to the past. Everything thus happened between two beds, one single bed and one double bed. Marriage is an event of closure. In its way it is one of the names of death: it is always recounted in the historical past. They married; they crumbled into dust.

★

I said: it's good that you're coming; and not: it's good that you're here. What I wanted was therefore not presence, not the staying, but the repeated coming, the present of trust and appearance, the time of the desired, renewable eruption, the limitless future of the recent past. Besides, the present is the tense in which he puts all his questions, which almost always involve an essence, a nature, or a place: if his questions are added up, altogether they reveal a sense of questioning that tends to rule out all the landing strips where I could bring down my darkness—once and for all he has taken off, he is living vertical to our common place, above this bed whose folds I carefully smoothed out just a while ago. As for myself, I know that when I answer him I'm filling out a questionnaire that he's left blank so that I'll fill in with my words what he means: thus, by answering him, I try to be his style, I listen to the silence swell after his question, as I would read with my fingertips if I were blind, and all I have to do is follow those traces with my eyes closed.

★

I often dream that I'm standing at the front door of a house to which I'm trying to attract him; the door is located on a strange little street, a tunnel with protruding walls (bulging arches at the base of a cathedral whose dome, red as a breast, I perceive as I lift my head, and distended front porches). This is not the main door, it's the service entrance, whose distinctive quality charms me so much that I'd gladly live there rather than in the modern anonymous apartment that I can't get myself to go into in the dream. It is made of glass and seashells, information that fills him with a certain curiosity, since, says he, they don't make them like this anymore. We are there. The door is my height. The doorjamb is fairly encrusted with seashells; the central section is of leaded glass: first of all a perimetric band of glass in that Virgin blue that dazzled me in Chartres years ago, the center is milky white or perhaps a very pale yellow, but as soon as the eye settles on it, it discovers that it's instead made of frosted granular glass of the type used for doors of secret rooms, those in which one wants to get dressed without being seen. I point out at the top of the door three holes in the glass, an inch or so in diameter, clean holes that have left no cracks, only simple crater-shaped splayings around each orifice. This door has been shot at; I deduce that these are traces of the War of '39, he maintains it's more recent. All this being of no importance, though, for what I wanted to share with him was simply this beach where his voice, as it dwindled, had left in my ear some points of reference. I, like seashells, knowing that I'd complete what he had to say, which he describes himself with the expression "a weighty question of love."

"Why ask it?" (I ask this because these questions are always in the present and charged with their own answers.)

"So that your answer might bring forth what exists and make it grow."

I'd like to persuade him to live with me in this house whose back door is bordered with imported blue glass, but he is rather reticent./

★

Does he know, when he questions me, that I am not here? He comes from Saturday, the way I saw him then, in the dresser mirrors, smiling at my smile, but then that smile referred back only to our images of desire; we laughed over putting on costumes, while in our real eyes we were passing over the walls that lay scattered toward a new world. No one was around. Who knows which garden he has stayed in since that time. I remember I was there, so long ago, and I'd like to get back there. But I fell between two days. If I fall, he's going to look for me. Out of his thousands of forces, there is one that can bring me back. He has to find the right force. As it stands now, it's good that he's bending over me and saying my name four times. Four is a good number. At the fourth call I open my eyes and begin to move. Again, again, it is necessary for him to call me, again, again, it is necessary for you to come, again, again, everything depends now on his perseverance, I revive, someone has let go and my limbs move about freely, so now it's all up to him, he has to come a little bit farther; then I'll be able to. Don't let go of me with a single word!

"Do you know what is limitless?"

I was leaning against the glass door at a fragile point in such a way that it suddenly shattered with an unheard-of

61

sound of a thunderbolt clap, sharp cries of glass, smashing of vertebrae, horrible crash of an almost human body, explosions of the senses that destroy the myth of the trail followed: for from now on we shall be able to pass from the center through everyone in every direction, nodes of truth tacked up in every corner, even those that are most closed off to memory, and to my eyes. Fulgurations that leave not a stick untouched, everything is wrapped in a light that takes all stealth by surprise, the most ordinary scenes are split wide open by unheard-of scenes of violence; ended are the ceremonies, the carefulness, the concessions; the curtains go up in flames, the burnt eyelashes fall from my eyelids into the hollow of my neck; blood flows in Pompeii, permeates the dried-out beds and dead veins. Pompey rises up; I am Caesar run through from every side, I take delight painlessly in the twenty streams of blood. But, my sensible memory says, Caesar is not a woman, is not you: that's pointless—here in the very powerful light of our eyes, there is no limit, Caesar is of use to me to spill my blood which is red.

What is limitless?

I almost didn't come back, because of the order of our discourse; indeed, this question logically preceded my exclamation: it's good that you're coming. When the two sentences finally came into contact, mine and his, finally coupled together, the darkness broke, I was assailed by all my senses, and now the only way I'm convulsed is by long, regular tremors of prophetic vision. When I think that I almost took Pompeii for Santiago. One detail: the window of my room in the strange house with the glass door opens onto a raised garden-cemetery. I'm told that under the gray paving stones lay the bodies of women who drowned for love; they are sirens; they've had engraved on the convex stone sweet accusations against men.

Oh, I see everything, I see everything, light trickles from my pupils, I bathe all the bodies, those that have lived, those that are living. I am tormented by my own power over a giant laugh. Carry the world with me, my love, who carried me in your flesh when I could no longer see. Why did Professor Hanold have to go so far to find his beloved who lived on the same street as he did in Germany? And why did Kleist have to invert high and low so far from Spain, which is so far from Germany? And what is the land or sea that I had to go across between Saturday and Monday?

I see everything, light is at the bottom of the waters, things at the bottom are dazzling.

In the detail of the dream, it is the sirens who perish by drowning. Elsewhere, it is said that they are the drowners. And in my mother's country, on the edge of the Rhine, they push men into the river. All these countries and these beds are far off, I've forgotten them.

Here in the present of our findings endlessly recounted between him and me, I didn't want to summon forth that which doesn't exist; he wanted to go ahead, I stopped him, he wrote down his name and I erased it. They tried to separate us, my love, the sea and dust tried to take me in, I almost took you for dead. Dead, you would have been my death. As it is I was sleeping without dreams other than of my body; and your living tongue woke me up. I was in mourning and you removed my veil. Listen, I hear everything. Truth is beating the drums, it's saying to me: "This is limitless. Your living body is limitless. You are the bow that shoots me and where I land you quiver. Space is not somewhere else, not smashed to bits, I'm not falling into its tombs, it is here from me to you, from you to me; we move about from hour to hour, from knowledge to memory, from night to day, without any limit inside our infinity. Our surface is the sun of our depth. We are the sea. The vessel is where we cross your questions and my answer. Speak and I know. Always you are coming."

"Where do you feel there is no limit?"

"Over there where he comes with his body. It's not a habit, it's a miracle, it's a coming with no previous departure, the absolute present that no thought, no being, no death, no world predicted, the total present where I see everything at once, spread out so perfectly that I embrace it with a glance: what can be seen can also be foreseen; Germany is our Chile, there is nothing that I didn't already see two thousand years ago today; this foreseeability creates the everyday unexpected for us, our imagined unbelievability, this meltdown of space folded back against our bellies, reversible."

"Why do you want my body?"

"First and last of all, I go through it to get to you. I turn it into the flesh and skeleton of my soul. Above all, no primal couple, no engendering pair, no reproductive function. I want to be an only daughter and virgin and gullible. At every moment I want to be able to go into that body, into that thought, at every moment be able to be before him as before a temple wall that doesn't exist, that exists only if I cross the wall and if I'm the door. I cannot 'do without' your altogether different body, which I never left in the first place. He's making me make millions of loves, it's not me, it's not my father. All the mysteries are there: I see my bones through your blood, I am in front and yet I am inside, I am the gaze and its abolition. I know that one much better than my own body, that one is the form of my organism, the concrete, the world gathered together, the prolongation of my consciousness, the passageway of my hope."

In the present of absolute vigilance, he responds with a whisper to my question:

"When I'm in pain, you cry?"

"Yes, when I'm in pain you cry."

"When will I cry?"

"One day I shall cry, I will have found our tears."

At these words I cannot hold back my tears: I hear him say the word "tears" and, like a heartrending *lectio divina* that would be delivered by his voice in my imagination turned into lover's face—in tears—this word spreads over my tongue, as far back as my throat, as a bitter, yet sweet, continuation; he makes his senses reverberate, at first breaking loose and seeming to evaporate, then recombining as a threat that clutches my throat and puts the fear of death in me; alarms, arms, blades clash around our souls, I'm afraid. An aftershock lifts Pompeii under my feet; I almost lay down on my side in the corner of Meleager's house. If you do not come, I'll be dying there.

I can tell him everything: how I lost him in the dust, how love kept away, how words wouldn't come anymore—and how I wasn't touched by that—and how all I felt was the increase in weight; I unbalanced myself by speaking to him. The story of this nothingness is nothingness. Deliverance is coming soon, I have nothing more to explain. Word is out.

Everything is settled.

Because of this long wait in an uncomfortable position my legs are numb, my thighs tense. He unfolds me and hoists me up, till I get back to my normal size, as well as the memory of our future, the amorous use of the bed and the structure of all movement. The joy of the joint: imagine a being without knees, without elbows, without desire. An egg. Then imagine the being released, bending, pliable, pleated, in circulation: we travel we change. His leg of mine.

If it weren't he, I wouldn't believe what he says to me: "Do you know that since Saturday your tongue has changed?" I wouldn't believe him, I wouldn't even understand him if it weren't he hence I. Do I know?

The word "deliverance" refers colloquially to the placenta. You have to let your tongue stick out for fifteen days.

★

He's supposed to come (arrive) at 2:15. Beginning at around 1:45 my body, starting to expect him, turns toward the door, my head tilts forward, my arms open, I feel him here already; I'm a hollow resonating with little joys.

At 2:15 he's not here, not yet, I'm not afraid, but everything dies down. I'm beaten down, enervated, without strength. A phenomenon that I'm beginning to be familiar with: if you do not come, I die.

At last, he has come. I've slept the five hours so deeply, impalpably far off, that speech returns to my lips only very slowly. He holds me, carries me, hugs me, lays claim on me— I wait. I smile. He kisses me, but I want to kiss him. I pull him onto the rug to kiss him, I tell him I want to kiss him, but he's the one who kisses me. I need to kiss him. It's not a question of a simple desire, of being excited, or of an impulse; rather, I am prompted by necessity to kiss him and thus to reproduce that nocturnal kiss whose meaning and agents I didn't understand, but which got caught deep down inside me in the form of need: precisely what one has to do to live.

/we were in a section of Venetian or Italian countryside, I'm not sure—I thought of Venice no doubt because, at the

bottom of a rather steep green-colored stairway whose landing we were stretched across, a canal was sketched out and
framed by a very high black wall also carpeted with wet moss.
On the right, halfway up, a sort of canvas-covered market
where people hold out trays on which merchandise is
arranged that's selling well (it seems designed for some kind
of creative project). And this is the action: I am bent over,
stretched out above a being on the point of dying, who is perhaps already dead but then who died just before, and I'm
resuscitating him. I don't see myself: in my place is a brisk,
white, diffuse fog endowed with senses, because I feel everything. I kiss the being lying beneath me. This kiss is in no
way an erotic kiss: it's an act of strength. I've got to wrench
the being away from death, bring him back to life. This being
bothers me, in spite of the extreme familiarity that exists
between us: he is long, thin, gaunt, black, and even though I
can in no way discern his traits (this olive-black, though, is
the color of the wall), he's at once feminine and masculine. In
any case, I do not hesitate to kiss him. Here's how I kiss him:
his mouth is open, I see it, wide open. In truth, it's rather the
black orifice by which I have access beyond, perhaps to land,
and through which I know I can get his breath back. I kiss
him, my tongue in his mouth plunges straight down, sucks,
labors, turning, restoring, this tongue is my tongue, muscular, powerful, exhaustible but faithful, trustworthy: it is
impossible for this thin, black, depleted hybrid being not to
come back to life. Although the success of my enterprise is
not yet clear, it is indubitable: though future, it is already
present, my powerful tongue of certainty. Now, I don't rejoice;
in some way this thin dark cylinder links up with ancient
pipelines along which I shed my tears of impotence once
before. What is a long, thin, black being, old-young, mascu-

line-feminine, neither man nor woman, neither dead nor alive, stretched out in a tomblike corner of Venice? (Hanold then proposes to Zoe that they take their honeymoon at the foot of the volcano. Another man would have taken her to the place where the canals run not inland in conflux but toward the sea in coagulation.)

That kiss is returned to me; I wanted to resuscitate him, I must. Now in my dreaming body incongruous sparks start to fly: I'm in rapture here where I'm laboring. If I experience this familiar yet displaced pleasure, cut off nevertheless from the Venice couple—for what I feel here is not taking place there—it's T.t. then who is stretched out black and emaciated, it must be him, it's got to be him; but only this burdensome, difficult black pleasure (the tongue is knotted, hardened, turgid, and, belonging less and less to me, cut off from my dreaming body; it resembles an arm, it plunges, it goes searching in the dark) makes me think that the being who is coming to—for an obscure puff of air passes through us, me as formless fog—that the anonymous being must have been a substitute for T.t. But as I regroup and dig and the hole becomes a crater, and as I come out of the dark to wait for T.t., it becomes clear to me that the being who has no form other than this black strip and this narrow, unfamiliar head, without eyes, without voice, without age, is the body of death. Did I kiss death so it could live? But it's in me that the fire is spreading. Did I catch it, am I going to die from it? Am I where I am? "What man dost thou dig it for, my friend?" "For no man, sir" "What woman then?" "For none, neither."

A few years ago I figured that out: my father was neither man nor woman. I saw him where I had left him while he was still a man, on a narrow hospital bed. That's where he vegetated between ages and sexes. Over the years he had lost senescence, he was lanky and weak, black and dusty; he didn't speak but he did look. His long hair grazed the floor. My mother would tell how he wasn't dead, but that, no longer having the force to live, he had withdrawn of his own accord. Happiness was my right eye, unhappiness was my left eye, how could I have seen him? I wanted to have a third eye that would never see him. And I didn't go up to him, I didn't touch him. I didn't kiss him, he wasn't dead.

Let our mothers bury our fathers.

He's not the one, this young black being, who needed to be kissed, who was between two places and could turn into coming to; I remember what was said by one of us, "call me by my name so I'll know you," but no name had been said. "Better to kill an infant in the cradle than to nourish an unsatisfied desire."

O my son my father my blood, weightlessly formlessly suspended above your limbs as a misty cupola, I must soon go through you and reach myself.

Was it death whose sky I formed last night? I didn't see myself. No face was revealed to me. Who died with no name, no sex, lying on his back in a raised corner of a city with green water? The being was lying down like that, on his back, the way he's lying down: he's suited to repetition. His head was placed on the sticky pavement in the southwest segment of the picture. His tongue came from the top and center. Like this. I take that shape; bending over I approach him, I am him. All at once I am not. Elsewhere has at last been granted to me, with the name, the sex of the being called forth, with the wicker cradle and the newborn child inside; with desire played out, mouth shut again, the black waters down the drain. "The head: Sublime," that was mine—that being that I wasn't and that no one was because it could be only me, but

I had no one to tell me my name. Who's kissing me? My tongue in the cradle, saved from drowning. "The genital organs: Beauty; the hands and feet: Proportion." I am recognized; I feel good. I am made. In a moment I shall get up. I am named tentatively *la Venise,* she who has come. How could I have said my name when I had no tongue in my mouth and the tongue I had was hanging down vertically, and I desired it?

★

The time has come to interrogate: what relation is there between my tongues? between our tongues? You ran into me. Our tongues intersected. This red land that I am needed your saliva; it brought me into the world with its teeth, it pulled me out of the ashes, it carried me in its flesh. He says: "The fragrance of your breath, if I were sleeping, would wake me up. If I were dead, I'd come back to life. Can you believe that?"

"I believe it, I know it."

We happen to have died already two times. The second time he was brought back by my breath; the first time I lost sight of him, lost my sense of him, lost his breath and flesh as well, but finally I saw him whole; I hated him, I was cut deep but in the end he pieced me back together.

★

We are familiar with terrors, doubts, black holes and white holes, eternal presences, primordial powers, the first waters and the last. At the intersection of our tongues there came to us a third body, at a place where there is no law.

★

Here is the chapter of the law: Your left eye you shall put out. Then you shall put out your right eye. Someone had spit in my face, and he wasn't there to wipe me off. How could I forgive him that spit? So I said to him: "Why did you spit in my face?" and also "Will you spit in my face again?" And he: "That can't be so important, just because I'm not there to wipe off your face." And I: "Someone spat in my face. And your words that were the fingers on your hands became knives."

"No, the words became your hands, your fingers. We can say any word."

"Come."

I say come. The word is said. The fingers on your hands are said, but I do not hear them. The spit speaks to the skin on my face. Will I ever be able to forget that? What's that going to do to us? Is that going to become ingrained in me? One wonders when this pain will stop hacking up my heart.

We walked one behind the other, I followed him and looked at nothing but his back, and I had forgotten that there existed things and a horizon. He was in front of me. I desired his face, his chest, the hair on his chest, the words on the fingers of his hands. I was enlightened. Someone spat in my face. My eyelids were running with the shit of the world, but he walked in front of me, he'd forgotten that there existed laws and groups, and he was in front of me, I heard him walking. How could I ever stop bleeding and flowing? I call to him, but my voice is blank. I ask someone to call to him for me. They pass him to me. They send him to me. He is a complement of an object. When I called to him, my voice was pale, but I saw him, he was of good height, taller than average, like a god figure. Objects must be seen as they are: we see they are small and insignificant in the face of human strength. The fiction is revealed. They send him to me.

He is sent, he looks at me. My face is running with our blood and with the shit of the world. The blow of the ax us has cut.

I am here, I have only to look in front of me to know what the word "distance" means.

How to continue in lockstep with him?

We are no longer a nesting of meaning and word. I am heavy and luminous and sulfurous. From where I am I see you. You are there where we used to be.

I am immense, I am monstrous, that ax outsized me. I have so little being and so much weight. What would I do with the sun today, I who sparkle with pain? You're losing my life. You cross over. This edge where you leave me doesn't border anything. Separation separates. Last night, what did I have my eyes open to? The moment I was going to call to him, upon him, I was caressing him with my eyes. Afterward, here's what I saw: I saw someone in front of him, really that's the way I saw it, and him behind, pretty far back, recessed, in the shade. That's what I saw, and I was in front, I was watching the way one watches one's nightmare.

The events flash by: Who will ever wipe off the spit? Who will destroy the house where I am not? Who will narrow the space between our sides? Who will return to me the shade of your body on my body? Nothing makes any sense, thing, being, no. Everything has no sense. There is too much death, not enough end. Where can be found, oh where the nameless force, is it the force of God-I-believe, is it the force of Self-I-make-myself-believe, where to find the outburst that causes no bursting, which way ourselves to get back, I don't know which way, I am here, I am before us, I lay siege to his body, our skin, how to go about this? What to say, and to whom?

To remain still as time passes, lying naked with eyes open, then when the time comes to close our eyes quickly one over the other, squeezed tight, so there's no more distance between the look and what is looked at; his body is my view, he takes the dead upon himself, and everything comes down to the same differences, which are these places where we run into one another.

You have to let your tongue stick out while the spit dries. Then he asks me for the strangest caresses: asks me to pierce him with my tongue here, and here, and here, and I pierce him, trembling in fear and from the effort, but it's out of me that the weeping blood comes. Lie across me, he says. I lie across him. I believe him. Time passes over our naked eyes; his eyes white, mine red.

Separation separates. Death is on the rise now—there's no more night—from it flows life. I want to sleep. I lean my back against him like Josephine with Jeronimo, but we're not carrying a child: each sees the other and impregnates him/her.

He puts his left arm around her as she turns her back to him, following the figure of Moses; she flows into him, she bathes in him, she molds herself to him till she's set, with his right arm he squeezes this found body that he wants to close in around. He wants her to go into him, to sleep in him, where the skin opens slowly it doesn't hurt us, there's no opening here, there's no slit or cut, there's the place where her tongue went through, on his chest. I slide down as he speaks to me. His voice is sweet and high, it comes from up above. He says: Have a dream of us. I must have ventured pretty far down. Predicate, I shed light on him, I talk about him from where I am, I affirm that he is very handsome. I add passionate qualifiers, I am positive.

★

Yet he said: Have a dream of us. That becomes an order here where I am. He has provoked me: Have it! he said, but he's the one who ought to, and I can only say what he does. I am only the tongue on which his thought settles. He summons me: Dream of us. I turn in the direction of us but in this turn I disappear, and I am expelled: for there can be dreaming, but there's no us; I wake in another place of sleep where I plunge again in the direction of us; I arrive at a lofty depth, a faraway place from us whence I begin to enact visually the history of the body: I hasten, I rush and remember, I see the body I have been since the beginning, through and through, I'm there, and though the body seen from here is gigantic, I see it from all sides at once, which takes for granted that I am the gigantic eye of God.

But seeing him from all sides, gigantic, whole, outside, his skin peeled, then rolled up, inside where everything is dark and red, I'm not up to it anymore. I am not the dreamer of us. I am in a dream that encloses a dream, I am the skin of the dream and I dream that skin, I am the outside of the inside, the eye that sees itself seeing everywhere, he is the gigantic master, the enactor of the Law, I am the edict that is established. Very quickly a modification is produced in the grammar of the dream. The being does not move. He is very handsome. Is. The subject, according to whether I look at it with an even eye or an odd eye, is masculine or feminine: it depends not on the being but on the eye. According to. When the subject is seen with an even eye, he takes me into his arms, he turns into heaven, he lies over me in an arc, he is all appearance. The pleasure of seeing the surface of his naked or molded chest through the skins of tight sweaters, a curved and modeled wall to reassure me.

When it's with an uneven eye that I watch him, he gives in to my desire without resistance: inside the flesh is the singular feminine common noun of our limitless existence; set down in the cavity, moistened, stretched out, eyes closed, I let whoever materializes do what he/she will, to the point where masculine and feminine can no longer be distinguished. Literally now, He is She, She is He; he—or—she is the blood and marrow of his, her beauty. Is is God, is he or she a giant, seen with the eye—one from all sides. Who says: "Detach me, separate me from being, so that my tongue can go in and out, hunt me"? There are resplendent moments when we no longer know which of us is the mother, which is God.

★

My mother has an important name. The name is Eve. My mother is still living. She is primordial, she is unforgettable. She is at times my daughter, so she slips on my clothes that are a little too long and too tight for her. She has this smile: I used to beg her to get up and turn the light on for me. Her mother calls her Eva, Eva, E'va. In the *Gradiva* the mother isn't spoken of: mothers are forgotten, perhaps never existed. It is true that the girl walks through Pompeii like somebody created out of stone; she slips into the walls that the earthquake has cracked, she appears and disappears under the watchful gaze of the archaeologist. She has a father whom they stumble upon by chance, while he's crawling on the paving stones encrusted with signs in the arid streets of Pompeii.

The Gradiva comes out of the walls at noonday going peacefully to nourish herself in the sun, mixing the heat and the bread, her body well within her folds, her face tiny, her eyelids unmoving, closed over a stowed thought. Only her lips move, she's chewing, one hears the insects humming and the Gradiva's jaws gently crunching. She is a young person who does not scorn food. She has nothing to do in Pompeii.

I, Gradiva, lively, active daughter of a father who spends his time creeping as close as he can to the ground that he digs with his fingers, with his eyes, with patience, for hours, at times motionless, lifeless torso confused with the columns, waiting for the desired creature to come out, I know by heart the amorous graffiti that have been scratched into the plaster of living Pompeii.

The real name of the young German woman begins with Z. Her father is a zoologist; she thinks that her mother wanted to please the learned man and be pardoned for being a woman or being around, and for that reason tried to pass the child off as an animal: otherwise why, when Zoe learned to recognize the sound of her mother's voice, did she find out that the first names they called her as a baby were those of little animals, bird, mouse, sparrow, turtle, Spatz, Mücke, Fliege, Biene, which filled her with fear at the idea that it's very hard to tell one mite from another with the naked eye, and perhaps her mother named her Zoe so her father would acknowledge her, get close to her, study her?

What are the Gradiva's childhood memories?

She remembers that she liked to torture animals, taking as long as was necessary.

What is she doing in Pompeii? She's walking at a pace similar to the flight of a large bird.

She goes through houses and temples, she slips through the chinks in cracked walls. The houses of Pompeii seem oblivious to the use of doors.

Did she love the young archaeologist?

Yes. Yes, because he had known her in the past by name, and because he had forgotten her, because she was completely crazy. Because he is upright and a fairly elegant young man, because he's marriageable.

★

My mother busies. She swarms. She comes at things from all sides. That lasts a few days, at the end of which the swarming is replaced by blossoming out in various ways. Neither days nor traces are counted any longer. She gains territory. She is numerous.

"You're coming at me from every which way," I say.

"So that's it? Now your father has been outdone?"

"The dead don't do anything. You scratch, you grate, you pop out of every chapter."

"To find where I am, you really have to dig."

"I've really loved you, you know."

"Yes."

"Remember that I learned passion from you."

She was the one I was waiting for. She would get up early, but I was already up: crouched in front of the door, I waited for her. The door didn't move, it was still there. I didn't know if I was in front of or behind the door. I wept. My unhappiness was daily and infinite. It didn't hurt. Crouched down, I watched the ants go from one cove molding to the next, infinitely, and I cried down over them. Some died by drowning. A death that doesn't hurt. They were never the same ants since they died by going from the molding into the water. But she was the one I was waiting for. She would have that smile. When? I was full of water that wanted to flow, of cries that wanted to pierce. There was flowing, there was crying, until not a single iota of unhappiness was left; and so it died away. I was dead for a time; I knew I was dead because during that time it made no sense whether she came or not. It made no difference anymore. So she too was dead.

★

I tell T.t. about how I learned about love back then, by adoring my mother. For a long time I believed the reciprocity was implicit. But I was the one who had chosen her, every day I chose her out of all human beings. It wasn't difficult, either; I recognized her by her smile. She hadn't chosen me. I have a good eye: I could have picked her out in a crowd. I flattered her, I caressed her, I followed her, I wooed her, I extolled her. She would look at me out of the corner of her eye, twisting her neck, very quickly. I didn't know if she was tall or short. She was beautiful. I didn't know that she was a woman. Beauty was what she was. She told me: a mother is always beautiful. I believed in the Law. A mother must be beautiful; what makes a mother is Beauty. The Beautiful is always mother. Is a beautiful woman always a mother? Between Eros and biology, the child has no place. I was her beloved, I was Jeronimo, for me she was unique and a virgin, I would take her in my arms, caress her, as if I knew the secrets. When I became her sister, I stopped using her ascribed name and called her Eve.

So when I happen to call T.t. "my beauty," I'm not creating any confusion, I quite understand that he's still King; for several months I resisted the desire to call him by that name sometimes; yet there are moments when T.t. is my mother, he knows, or else my origin, or my life's finery.

Exuberance is the Beautiful. The Beautiful is too much— that accounts for its ripping apart: when there's not enough room for it to come out, the Beautiful rips through, it's capable of killing. If I had held back my Fair Love, I would have suffocated. I had only to see Eve for the words to spring forth from every direction. We have mouths all over our body. Words come out of our hands, our underarms, our belly, our eyes, our neck.

Let's return to the King, whom I call "my beauty," who is at times my mother, at times my child. This chapter is that of the Counter-Birth. Everything takes place here upside down and against the law of nature and society, in this place where life and death have equal value so long as death wishes to be life, so long as life consumes itself till it dies. One comes here rarely. Some get here by accident. Imagine a beautiful woman, a young widow, faithful to the memory of the handsome husband she lost three years before, and who is pregnant; and imagine that this young, faithful, pregnant widow is dearer to you than eyesight, that you've mourned the husband's death as if he were your brother or yourself, and that you know this young woman as well as if she were your daughter or yourself. Or: you're sleeping, the night before you had gotten into bed with a clear conscience as if that day were to be your last, and imagine that it's not the daylight that comes to bring you the new day, but a dream that awakens you—you dream that you're carrying a child in its fourth month, and this dream violently recalls to you the vigilant sorrow of your widowhood. This dream seems to you to be the bearer of something impossible that might have been possible, and fills you with a nostalgia for living that agitates you and settles in your breast, as if your womb itself were moaning and convulsing. At this same time, pain suddenly overthrows your reason and takes advantage of the disarray of your senses to usher in the inverted logic of a mad desire: a second dream intersects with your pregnancy dream in the form of a visitation declamation. As you stand in a torrential sunlight, a wind of beating wings carrying you, lifting you, annulling the weight of your body where the second body is living, you say to yourself that this discovery of a life in your womb, far from being the sign of madness or of regret, is on the contrary the proof that what you've taken for reality is this: a three-year widowhood which is the dream from which, finally, the living truth is tearing you away. For if the child moves, it means he's living; your body has already carried a child three times and recognizes those abrupt, intimate caresses. And the reason there's a child inside you is that you had that frightful dream of a burial, and now it turns out he's not dead, it is thus the child who tears away the funeral veils and returns to you the husband who you believed, out of terror and superstition, was dreaming of death. Is there any dream more sovereign than the one which kills death and snatches from its monstrous bosom, unwilling to release them, those beings it believed it could keep there? Is there any more overwhelming joy than that of resurrection? And any news more sublime than that of birth? Thus through the reversal of pain and of its reasoning, this unknown infant is the one to bring his father back into the world. The father might in this way be the son. And if now you've been pulled out of the second dream by the very thing that gladdens your heart and reassures you and makes you laugh at your nocturnal anguish, if the infant rolls in his ship and draws you out of the repose into which you had slipped the night before in a state of purity, emptiness, and regret that makes you wish this day would end your life, and assuming you are lying here, eyes open, amid the folds of fine linens on your widow's bed, right where he used to lie in your arms no more than three years before, your body positioned in the way that had become your amorous habit, in the exact hollowed-out place of his last night, in your bed of faithfulness along the very trace of your sole night of death, right there where he was stretched out in your arms enclosing his head, you not wanting to shut the eyes through which you implored him, distraught by this point, to let your soul enter with him into his death, because his lips no longer wished to admit your tongue, your breath, the way they had done even yesterday, familiarly, indulgently, so easily that at times you even threw him on the corner of that mouth, today impassable, a tiny, light, offhanded, timeless, blind kiss, and right there where by the end of the night his eyes stopped taking you in, they no longer returned your image, they killed you, they repudiated you, you were no longer the apple of his eye, you were already erased from his memory and you thought you'd die seeing yourself turned away by those pale globes that could no longer bear your tears—then you hated the eyes that even yesterday you adored, light gray, veiled only by passion, suns, nourishment of your eyes that had been turned inside out, indifferent, offering now only their distracted aspect to your pressing need, white sterile eggs fattened by billions of aborted looks. And you had envied that body that was leaving you in the world as it turned away from it. His eyes had been sunshine gray when he looked at you. At the sight of these pale eggs you thought you'd die, but you just fell asleep on his silent chest. From that sleep you awoke alive and widowed.

And out of this sleep you are now drawn by the one who moves, more widowed, more alive, more frightened, less lonely. You are lying down, eyes open, on your back, in the exact same hollowed-out place where he left you. And you think you're losing your mind or else your life, for what is cannot be; for it to be, you must be the faithful widow that you believe you are, and yet you mourned him three years ago, and you believe you are the same woman today as the one who mourned, and yet how could you be a widow and pregnant and faithful to your mourning? You'd lose your mind trying to be at once faithful and pregnant, or perhaps you're having a third dream, but if you hoped to be dreaming again, your womb is not dreaming, your body is not mistaken, nor are your eyes that do not deny the repeated appearance of a slight swelling that moves around on the waistline of your belly, yes, flesh has an undeniable memory, it's not tricking you, it would never put you off the track, but it prophesies the near future, it gives you a sign that it's going to unravel the proof of the existence of the Invisible.

On the one hand Too much. On the other Not enough.

And Too much is Not enough.

On the one hand the bed, the woman inside, the infant inside.

On the other hand, nothing, a hole in time, blank eyes, empty space.

The bed is in the still young room, with acoustic curtains, full of flowers and living plants, where the sunlight makes the dust particles dance, a well-known room, indubitable. In the room the bed is for two.

Religion, society, the law should throw the young widow into a dangerous state of anxiety. Aren't the facts her enemies? She is neither virgin, nor godly, nor mad. She is pregnant and a widow, and Reason, which she respects just as much as her father, has become her enemy, because: it is impossible for a dead father to beget a child, it is impossible for a child to be his own father; it is impossible to be faithful and pregnant. Biology, the chemical sciences, the laws of probability denounce the young woman. There is no man who is not born of a man. End of discussion. And beginning of the child.

Any person other than the Marquise von O. would have accused the intangible powers, science, faith, the law, reason, rather than giving in to the evidence of the tangible: the tangible is the fruit of the tangible.

Kleist tells how the Marquise von O., finding herself pregnant by accident, made it known through the medium of the press that, without explaining how, she was with child and that the perpetrator was to appear, in order to make himself known and to acknowledge the child. Kleist gives none of the names of the characters, out of distrust of religion, of society, and in general of the priests of Blame, so that their descendants would not pay today for the faults of yesterday. The body and soul of the Marquise von O. lived in Edenic harmony: the presence of a third party, far from hampering their union, enriched it. The marquise's soul even welcomed this unexpected guest, never doubting the good faith of this body that had at one time been of such good use to her. Guilt could not make a dent. Never had she been so faithful.

T.t. and I, one day, will be dead. Then you will know. But we know, as of now, and that's why we live on the intangible line that separates this side from the other, this death from our life.

The Marquise von O. loved the infant before he appeared on the intangible line, during the time when he knew nothing, for the following reason: through him her suffering would be eliminated, a suffering that, out of all suffering, was the most all-consuming, caused by the blotting out of her image in the eyes that till then had brought her light and made love with her. Since those eyes had spurned her, approaches made to her and incursions of any kind were repugnant to her, for she no longer had to seek constantly the sources of life, she had only to go on blindly, till the end, outside of all the mysteries that it was vain from now on to wish to penetrate. She had not entered into the lie of duplicity, she had not tried to separate love from the love-object; so as to continue loving love beyond the dead object, she had accepted the most solitary of solitudes, that in which the memory doubles the present of a past that does not toy with the actual mirror. Love was empty like the bed. Her eyes could not invent for themselves another mystery. The eyes of the living, moreover, were already filled with other images, places, memories, figures of desire: her mother saw in her the image of her father, and her father saw himself in her— she wasn't seen straight on or as a unique individual. But there would be those eyes that would take her, call to her, reproduce her with each blink; and in exchange she would serve as a primal threshold. She was eager to see him. He would be entirely new. There couldn't be a more direct sort of love. That's the reason she didn't feel like playing the couples' guessing game: since the infant was unique, unconnected to any lineage, an absolute birth, it didn't matter to her if it turned out to be male or female. The infant was life. He would have no accounts to settle with anyone, no one to resemble.

★

We look at each other at times, lying on our sides, motionless, eyes open and stupefied to be two people in the

84

process of exchanging being: the one I see is more me than I am myself. At that moment there can exist no purer or more direct love. So we think: are there times when we "understand" our love? We understand it when we've stopped understanding it. Just as the yet unborn child has no sex, so we understand our love when we no longer know how to understand who we are. So we can be born, but not at the same time, or in the same way. Eve has been here for a long time; we know that time is a relation between two beings. When Eve is here, I no longer exist, I'm in hiding, sometimes I even remember myself. Eve is multiple and primordial. She spreads out, she spares no room, she desacralizes, check stubs punctuate my books, the space is stripped of partitions, doors fall, I am cornered, I am without secrets, I sacrifice everything on the limitless altar of my mother. T.t. and I thread our way along the crevices.

★

Eve is my mother's real name. T.t. is a made-up name. I should have used it a long time ago, but I hesitated because of its symbolic overdetermination. It's a clumsy name, of bad amen, yet it's the name of radiant mourning, of tenacity. I must avoid probable confusions: I never saw myself in Isolde, I am Tristan.

My name is impossible to pronounce, that's why I don't give it. Besides, T.t. never uses it: during all these years I've never heard him try to say it a single time. That proves that I am not the other: I remain in the kingdom of his being, without being subject to it or an attribute of it. I am the center and the limit of his kingdom, the skin of his existence, by which he breathes and protects himself. I have this encompassing gaze on him that procures for the body, in this case his, the

85

sensation of seeing itself very closely, the turned-in outside envelops the inside like a glove. Eve has used exclusively my name since I became an adult: because her native language is German, she has a certain hoarseness, a muscular breathing, a rising and falling that thrust me into a variegated, mountainous landscape. She knocks me down when she summons me: she exhales me, she blows me to extinguish me, she chops me up, she "achs" me, she steams me, clouding the mirror in which she doesn't recognize herself. My mother stays a long time. She dreams that she takes my car, inside of which there is a baby, hers, born of a father she does not love and who must have impregnated her with a kiss given on the street corner. But it's good to have a baby at her age! She parks the car haphazardly, rushes into a bank, overwhelmed with fear, comes back to move the car which she finds has been crushed, a scrap heap onto which she sheds tears. In digging through the heap she finds the child alive under the sheet metal, his mouth sealed shut with a little iron bar.

★

"Love me, bring me into the world," I say to my mother. She wants my life, she wants my death, she wants my body reduced to silence.

There's no more room here for me, papers endowed with willpower increase and multiply, my hand extends, she gives me money, she comes at things from all sides, she ascends, she fills up. I knock down the sixth wall in extremis and T.t. hoists me up out of the mother. Where to go? T.t. says that we're going to leave, that we're going to create the world, that we're going to discover everything in ourselves, that we're going to we we we. I'm frozen with fear, or with cold, I don't know. I know I, no more. No, I say, I don't want us to leave.

"What? You don't want us to leave? To find ourselves? To be ourselves?"

"I don't want to want anything. I want you to want. I've come undone. Do for me."

My mother calls T.t.: the good T.t.

He says: "You know very well that we're the ones who do everything; you are us just as I am. We do for ourselves."

"Nanny [*Nounou*].* Nanny. I don't know anything, I don't want to know anything. I. I've got to learn everything. Do for me. Know for me. You. Born of us? No, of you. I am to be made, everything is to be made. No we. No first majestic couple. I have a navel, I'm attached to it, and for my part I value it; tie me up or cut me loose, do for me; I have a loathing for the smooth belly of the woman not born of a woman, and who therefore has no memory only a curiosity, and who has no back only a face. No we! Later, later, later. Are you willing to do for me first? I am hindered, outdistanced, look for me, push me on."

"Yes, I'm the one who shall carry you forward and I shall do for you." Gigantic, he picks me up and puts me in his pocket. I am the pocket woman of God. Take your time, take your time, I don't let people have their way with me so easily. This living God who puts me in his pocket is not the dead God. He can therefore have a future and understand everything. He moves forward, I follow. We walk fast, at times slowly. When he gets closer, I slow down so as to maintain the right distance between us.

★

*Play on *Nous nous faisons*, the previous sentence; hence echo of the words for "we" and "ourselves."—TRANS.

How to outwit the aggressor? One pretends to go up against a resistance equivalent to the thickness of a wall that a stubborn ram crashes into over and over again. Then one gives way, suddenly vanishing, and the aggressor who had collected his forces for the attack is hurled forward headfirst into the void he's rushing toward. The idea that my mother might not have filled the house up to the brim hadn't occurred to me. Silently, already broken, crammed down, repapered, to provide less surface for her gesture, I opened the doors. A mouselike nature. That filling to the brim was not entirely inauspicious. Having been sent away, I turned now with all the more energy toward T.t. Bitter taste of childhood, of orange sucked in hiding, of sweets secreted under the beds, of offenses magnified by hatred and love, my mother's two discrete breasts. Walls everywhere. On the walls graffiti of frustrated lovers. I love T I love you. Displaced excitations of a wandering adulterous couple. A delayed adolescence. I the child martyr of my mother's loves as I waited to witness mine, later.

Mother to my mother, mother-daughter and grandmother, I hustle myself, I procure. I am too young, I am too old. I say:

"I hope you slept with him."

"Only one time, the first date."

"Was it good?"

"Not bad."

"Then why only one time?"

"That was enough for me. I haven't been broken in enough. A woman of my age is well advised to take every precaution."

"Age is a fiction."

"It plays a big part, especially with men, and there was a certain combination of circumstances. I had died with my slippers on."

"How about me, how old do you think I am?"

And how old does T.t. think I am, and how old do I think I am? At every second the age of ignorance the age of knowledge; after each embrace the age of God. But we'd been living for days like suckling infants.

The door with the orange-colored tiles gives way and we fall right after the discharged waters, headfirst, like two twins who are well-engaged.

★

The vice-regal palace was swallowed up, the tribunal where the fiery death sentence had been pronounced was, in place of the building, nothing more than a churning basin of hot red waters, the mother superior had perished crushed under a rafter, there was not a single wall standing in the town, people didn't know if they were coming or going as they passed across the gutted foundations. A new age arose out of the gaping entrails of the era that was over. A new human nature appeared that was vaster, more open, more similar to divine essence than the crushed race had been, monumental and harmonious, a living edifice of regular proportions, with mighty stamina, welcoming to the wretched, temples of protection and not seats of Judgment and Execution. They couldn't believe their eyes: they felt their arms, their legs, their necks, they made their peace with the present, thinking they had dreamed the time of walls and the eruption.

The Gradiva shares a piece of bread with the archaeologist, and this bread is edible, it exists. Therefore the Gradiva nourishes herself with bread, as do humans. Her mouth opens, closes, she chews, she swallows. Her jaws are heard crunching. T.t.'s lips touched my lips, therefore we weren't separated. Let those who have never given birth not take the following event as a parturition: there was no child; on the other hand, there was a violent wave passing through my mother whose signs were new and ungovernable; I became the locus of a natural phenomenon unknown to me, and its extraordinary feature was this: the unleashed passion that was in every respect an integral part of the totality of my body was a force way beyond my control, my bones groaned at being still held together, my flesh moaned at being solid, everything wanted to be blood and all my blood wanted to have as a vessel not just the narrow canal system that fed me, but the universe, all the energy, sensations, aspirations, terrors, thirsts, plunged down into the same gorge; the whole course of my life turned round by the eruption of this monstrous torrent swirled into a boiling lake from which red vapors rose, and this lake also absorbed flesh, water, forms, an inverted volcano that would never stop swallowing up, hollowing out an eager belly, impelling, gaping, digging out to the point of threatening to burst. Never would I have been a match for this; not only was I overwhelmed, decentered, dismembered, a gulf and engulfed, but what's more, the terror that I felt was all at once swallowed by a greater terror: I feared an interruption of the catastrophe which had become the epic form of my existence; all at once this terror was consumed by the fear of succumbing, and thus from one terror to the next to the point of the systematic upheaval of everything that exists: the summit plunged into the infinite depths, the end opened up to the beginning, life wanted to know death, and I wanted T.t. to help me hurt myself. Now, at the moment I asked him, perched as I was on the edge of him as on the edge of the desired abyss, either because I clumsily overturned this flaming cauldron onto him, or because, unable to hold up the cracked edifice of my terrors, I crushed him under it, he shrank away under my gaze, crushed, frightfully squashed, bereft of all warmth and substance and language.

In a sense this fainting acts in the short term like outside air on the lava, finally congealed, which sticks to the sides of the volcano. Now we are devastated, nothing moves anymore, and extinction would be sweet, if T.t. could only speak to me. But something somewhere holds him back, in a place whose point of entry I do not know and where he wants to stay. Under my gaze his eyes grow distant, his body in my arms does away with its natural weight, and effortlessly I can lift him up. I carry him: the air was a body of water; there, where the air is water, is revealed counterlove, love from the other side that knows neither right nor left, neither woman nor man, neither age nor death, neither regret nor diminution. T.t. thought he would die for not being the abyss I wanted to fall into, for being on this side when I was tilting toward the other side. His eyes were closed to me, I leaned against his lips and called him. I asked him to return, I begged him to come back to me, to open up, I kept calling him by name, I drew him out, I promised him all the time spans, and yet I caressed him as though we were stretched out on the edge of our tomb, the last day: each word, each gesture, each invocation had the perfection of something that will never again be said, never again be done, never again be called out, of something that will have no succession. I was a goddess and I was touching the god. We crossed History, his memory and mine, the blue waters and the red waters, and I was just about out of breath, for I had kept on carrying him, when at last I sensed his eyes crossing the deserts to come back. Lying on my side, calm, patient, gigantic, I hold him tight, his eyes have returned, his eyelids are poised on the first questions;

I've been carrying him for months and now he looks at me; I look at him, and we no longer know who we have been. At that precise instant of counterbirth we are granted a third body through which we come into being. It enters headfirst.

★

Count F. is a man of action and passion. Kleist shows him engaged in a destiny so rapid that the count never stands still during this brief instant we are permitted to see him. It is not necessary, moreover, to the functioning of the narrative and the series of explosions that make up the plot for us to see what he looks like. Count F., the Russian nobleman, is defined by the rhythm, the audacity, the strength, the exactingness of his behavior, by his constant challenging of natural laws, of the laws of Chance, of the laws of honor and society, by his brilliant victories. He waits for nothing, he takes, he's an attacker. His motives are as obscure in the eyes of men as those of an angel. He rushes all over in an immense gesture of destruction and of creation. He wants everything. He gets everything; the strong cannot hold out against him. Some secret plan spurs him on: his prodigious energy, his readiness, his way of turning time upside down and breaking through obstacles, of striking down, of brutalizing the event which he makes his slave, causes him to appear in the figure of an angel. We know he is young and that, whether because it reflects the fire at the citadel that he took so quickly or because it reflects the ardor of his blood and the speed of his emotions, his color rises all the time. Now, this man who is a delegate of life forces, who saved the Marquise von O. by tearing her delicate body out of the ignoble hands of ruffian soldiers, bashing their bestial faces to pieces, who took the fortress in the course of a Monday, is mortally struck down by a bullet in his chest on Tuesday. That made clear that he wasn't an angel. The seat of passions shatters when hit by a bullet. Certain beings whose life is absolutely over and above the norm do not assume their human form until the moment when death strips them of it. Nothing is more unbearable to the heart than the death of an immortal. Because of that, because of the symbolic beauty of the angel of war, the Marquise von O., whose trust had not been defiled by the nonetheless distressing death of her husband, felt the greatest pain: the death of Count F. at the dawn of his omnipotence was a sign of God's mills whose grinding spared none but the spineless and the foolish. It made her experience the sharpest kind of anguish: if Life could be demolished by Chance, how could one not despise this toy loaned to man by a nonselective God? This was manifested by repeated episodes of discomfort in her whom people took for a goddess of health. The symptoms were as follows: nausea, dizziness, loss of energy, at times fainting, craving for and loathing of certain foods. It was as though the Marquise von O. held in her body the disastrous combat between life and its suppression, a combat that had touched her so deeply. Or rather, as though she, O., goddess of health, impregnable fortress, had become the location of a living memory. As though, in her revolt against universal History and Injustice, she had called upon her flesh to become a living memory and in so doing she had impregnated her own womb, a living and delicate tomb imbued with the angelic count's spirit. O. lived within the symbol with such clarity that she did not refuse the idea of a choice: that a superhuman nobility known to certain people she bore witness to in her very flesh. Her yearning for the Beauty seen in Count F. was so deep that she came to regret that he had died without issue. She dreamed of herself as a lake of fiery currents on which evolved a brilliant swan. The swan dove down, she wept, the swan came up. It was called Thinka. It dove down. She named it, so it came out of her own mouth. This swan became necessary to her. Thinka dove down, came back up, dove down with a violent oscillation that reproduced the count's leaps and challenges, a symbol of the martial rhythm of life. In the hurried sequence of events and amid the cries and the flames, she had never seen his countenance. She had seen only his flaming face.

She told her mother that if she had to give a name to the malaises, which in any case were not unbearable, she could do so only by comparing this internal agitation to the kicks made against the dark womb by a child, held inside, to be born. In saying that, she wasn't betraying the lost husband or her mother's sanctity or her mother's authority: the nobility of her nature was such that this marvelous yet tragic presence of a martial Beauty in her womb did not embarrass her. She was not pregnant, except by the angelic figure of Thinka. She even came to desire, in reveries that defied the limits and laws of nature, to be a strange, powerful goddess who could bring back to the world the vanished hero. If Count F. had, on that night from Monday to Tuesday, embodied immortality, the Marquise von O. bitterly upbraided herself for being mortal, for during this same conflagration when he had dismounted and crossed the palace to save her, scarcely had he rescued her from the peril when she lost consciousness. Thus, Count F. had given her a life that she had let go of. In a sense, that night, it was the count who served as god, father even. But aside from the Holy Virgin who had been the mother of God, no woman, no goddess could carry a God, or bring into the world a man already made.

The color of T.t.'s eyes when he swam on the ethereal lake, and as he came back to me across the blue waters and the red waters, was milky: it was that cloudy gray-blue that doesn't yet reflect the light but wants to drink it in, that color of origins that fades in the little child only at the end of the age of ignorance, when day begins to chase away the prenatal night, and it was the eyes of a little infant scarcely a few months old that questioned me, as I carried T.t. in my arms as though he weren't a man already made. Infant King, I said, come back, exist, marry me. And I rejoiced that my husband was also my son and that he entered me headfirst.

★

Instead of taking care of his daughter, the Gradiva's father crawled on the ground and had eyes only for the desired beast that would come out of the cracks. No sign of life in this desiccated Pompeii, where old Bertgang creeps on his belly, at the lower level of the universe, in that place where man is confused with the earthworm. His daughter comes back into his memory only when his insides demand food. The Gradiva is charged with seeing to the nourishing of her father. Her father's aim is to catch the lizard Faraglionensis by surprise if it comes out of its hole. He expects the lizard the way others expect the Messiah, the way the archaeologist hopes for the Gradiva, and the way the Gradiva awaits life. But in this field of desires, the lizard is the fascinating figure: by its manner of popping out and then disappearing, with its strangely rich colors, green and gold—fertility, wealth, by its infinite patience, that gift of prolonged immobility to the point of imitating death, by its eruptions abruptly cut off, by its mysterious contemplations of the void, and by its surrender to the sun—sometimes supple, other times rigid, by its vigilance in sleep and its indifference to man whom it came before on earth. Archaic.

This lizard has no apparent relation to Jensen's narrative. It has so little relation that its intrusion is indecent; if Hamlet found fat gray Polonius in Gertrude's bed, if he had seen him sneaking in between the folds of the sheets, if Jeronimo had thought to check whether his cloak had gotten a tear before spreading it over the Carmelite and the child, I would experience the discomfort provoked by a superfluous detail in the harmonious economy of a happy dream. This lizard is a luxury. The only excuse for it in my eyes is that it serves as pretext for the paternal creeping. The fact that Jensen slipped, through association, from the zoologist on his belly to the lizard's taut abdomen may mollify annoyed readers whose pace is slowed by making them contemplate the scholar at work. But the lizard is not only in a contiguous relation with the person observing it. It has a value in itself which is signaled by the color connotation: this absolute lizard, a perversion of the narrative, wants to be green and gold. It resists all interpretation, except that which attributes to him, beyond the syntagmatic pretext, an ironic function of substitution: we might say that from the zoologist father's viewpoint, the lizard takes the place of the daughter. The colors (in German *grün* and *gold*) would be at once natural and allusive because of the common initial letter G. Or else, the real name of the Gradiva being Zoe, the father behaves toward the lizard just as he behaved toward his daughter when she was not yet grown up. There remains Jensen's hypothesis: this father,

Bertgang, who has come to Pompeii to hunt the lizard on good advice and thanks to a new invention—an herb collar to catch the animal in when it comes out headfirst from its hole—is so absorbed in his quest that if he had to choose between the lizard and the girl, he'd leap for the lizard, as if the girl were nothing to him but air. The zoologist is stretched out flat on his belly at high noon under the sun on a slope at the foot of the mountain that overlooks Pompeii. In the slit of the rock shines the head of a lizard.

★

I knew in my childhood, the first one, that heat and that slope, and doubtless that lizard, too. It was in my first childhood, the childhood I think of rarely, though I'm often in contact with my second childhood. It took place in a town that was at the time full of commotion, mountainous, populous, athirst, humming: my father's town; that town disappeared during a cataclysm fifteen years ago. It disappeared, leaving no ruins. That head and that slope were in a pine grove that seemed like the hair of an enormous head-shaped crag, a natural sphinx that gazed intently at us, the people of this town on the edge of a body of burning blue water. It was said that there was a gold-covered church nestled behind the rock's neck, beyond the sunny slopes, but I never saw it. The head was called Santa Cruz.

★

I ask T.t. to read the *Gradiva*. The text being unavailable, I just set off effortlessly down the cobblestone avenues. Would I have had the right to go along here in the past, to drink from the public fountain, to bathe among the women? Here I must leave a blank space. I could refrain from doing so, but I have scruples about faking; I admit here that I forgot: first, when the lizard comes out for the first time; second, the textually exact first words addressed by the archaeologist to the Gradiva Rediviva and the language used at the time; I remember only that she answers in German, saying: "You must speak German." Here I leave a blank space. Meanwhile, the archaeologist has a dream of metamorphoses. But for me, it's essential that T.t. come back, for he is my memory.

And what color was the unique cloak that wrapped the trinity under the flowering tree in Chile?

★

I am in this room, a vestibule, which is neutral, and I can't see the walls, or the ceiling, or the floor, but it's defined by the geometric system of its molding. In this room, there is no time. I might have entered it recently, but there's a perennial quality to the air that suggests an undated oldness, not weighed down though by duration. I'm here with my mother. It doesn't seem as though we intend to leave. We show no sign of activity; a silent, unmarked complicity connects us. It is possible, moreover, that the presence of my mother, whom I do not see, is purely fictional. It is possible also that I am my mother. There is my mother. Do I have one sex? I have one I. No more. ONE calm, vibrant, attentive I. And now what I suddenly see at the extreme right of my field of vision: a mouse going into its hole. I don't see the mouse go into the hole. But it's the first bit of knowledge, the rupture in non-time. To say, as I do, that I see the mouse go into the hole is an ambiguous assertion, false and true: there is in me a deductive logic that I didn't know about, which by this abrupt manifestation introduces me into an already started time, teaching me that I preexisted that instant. However, there is no past in this room. But the future is already opening and plunging toward me. What I say is false: I don't see the hole which is blocked by a body, I see only its contour, like a gash in the wall, yet another eye sees the hole, black and substantial, but not a dead end. Let us consider set E and the set F(E) of its subsets (F being the letter that includes all the other letters; the set of the subsets, F is part of E). Among the latter A and B are disjoint. B is disjoint with respect to A but not with respect to C. Suppose Large A to be the set (E, A, B, C). Then the relation of inclusion defined by the elements of F(E) is a relation of nontotal order: A and B can be included in C, but C is not necessarily included in A and B. The relation is not reflexible but it is antisymmetrical. I see only the tail: therefore the head (A) and the body (C) have already gone in. And this gray tail, nacreous gray, mouse gray, which is going to disappear into the hole, is not a mouse tail. Broad, fat, and flat, this tail, unexpectedly noticed at the time when the body was already in, is nothing other than the eruption of the lizard into this colorless, timeless non-place! How can I express my rapture, the light that goes on in my head, the comic yet terrifying series of the most ancient signifiers that make my memory and my astonishment race down a gunpowder trail along the molding with no wall, continuing at the pure speed of lightning; delight of non-interruption, of renewal, of going back to the end; I no longer have and never did have a body to touch with my own fingers, and I have never seen my eyes in such a way that I could cross over to see myself: a violent realization, to which no offered resistance, for more than, I not ever had this I, but this light that I am is there, at one extreme; at the other extreme, *an andern Ende, amandernende,* one word that will be only mine when I get there, O rejoicings. Isn't the capital E at the end beautiful? (this might be a thought to make my mother E. settle down); so yes, if I exist, then E is the hole through which this light sweeps and returns—a light so white that I cannot see it, cannot touch it with my iris, for it blends with the ambient light that I use to see, therefore a light that must be referred to by its end, by its speed, by its sense of history. And also by this white joy that washes over me.

It empties in the end into water that is blue, still, dull, rough-textured, but translucent enough for the contours of things stuck to the bottom to be discernible and distinct. This bluish windowpane, chiseled with little waves, a vertical, pale, marine surface colored a solid blue scarcely distinguishable from white, formed the outside wall of the bathhouse our family used when we lived on S. Court, in a house that no longer exists today. The cabin had wooden partitions and was painted white with gray-blue spots on three sides, the fourth, a back window jutting out over the garden, was paneled with that rippled glass onto which branches of wisteria attached their tiny suckers. At the base of this invisible, far-off trunk of the plant there were doubtless different little insect colonies and batrachia. The round mirror in which I made faces at myself was hung in the center of this surface. Watching myself change from childhood to adolescence, I perceived out of the corner of my eye—the lizard. Warmed, it could remain motionless for hours on end, holding steady, legs spread, toes flat, tail stretched out at rest. It was about four inches long, thin and well-built. Gray no doubt, but I never went out to check: for eight years I lived in front of the lizard, which seemed gray. I never saw its eyes. It was an elegant lizard, thin and calm, with a soft belly beating with tiny pulsations.

Then it would vanish with a quick movement, head first (A), then the arched but unjointed body with long gray belly (C), the tail following, as though broken off, beast of the beast (B), thus A then C then finally B, A seeming disjoint from B, C taking B in tow. My father did his washing up leaning over the white sink, his back turned to the window of solid blue water. My father's back, the lizard's belly. I between the back and the belly, just now I look at my father's back, I know he's my father (F), we understand one another, or rather I am understood by him, and when he has his back turned, I examine him and try to understand him: this is my father's back, which is part of my father's body. The lizard ducks its head first across the pale still water. A placed before B (A < B) and B placed before C (B < C) is followed by tail ↓ etc.

All that seems so clear to me. The mouse without head or body is my lizard; the body is already inside as my dream is already in another dream that writes it. On the other side of the hole, through which the tail should enter, there's the place where it's being written. The lizard affair will have to be noted carefully and in detail: how the mouse (feminine gender) was the lizard (masculine gender). How my mother's presence was an absence. How the past was located at the endpoint of a line, the prolongation of the molding on the wall, represented here by the molding and the hole. How, three weeks ago, I refused to get a lizard belt for T.t. on the pretext that it was made from an animal. How I never saw the lizard except through the windowpane and I never thought of going around to see its back, whereas I did see my father's back. It's quite possible that its back would have been green and gold. How I did algebra, as well as German, with my mother after my father's death. Yes, you'll have to note all that, so that we understand it.

And finally, that command so forceful, so imperious, so playful too, drama, myth, battered door, laugh of the woman who's just given birth, of the dead man dying, that superb, outrageous password that springs forth at this instant of recording and, without spilling any blood, tears apart that hymeneal dream, and is said in a strong, loud voice, a vertical voice, eyes lifted toward the great accomplice in whom all the archives are engraved, in the voice of a son or daughter of God—for am I not either one or the other and isn't this voice the radiant sign that I am? LIZARD. ARISE!* A living, super-human phrase. The breaking of latency.

Lizard. The dream departs from the dream. I leave the dream departed from the dream, expelled headfirst, and I don't leave alone: following me are all the letters of words taken as a whole from a voice quite relevant to the oldest of my laughs. Lizard—arise! Who gave me this gift, who gave back to me the belly and the back? And the lizard and the wisteria, and inside the cabin, the bathtub in which I float no memory of my memory, the mirror into which all my forces plunge, and my naked father washing up.

I am asked what my father's name was: his name wasn't Lazarus, it was Georges. Son of Samuel son of David. No Lazarus anywhere. This is not about him. It's getting dark. Nor about chance. Nothing moves under the h.† Lizard—arise. Nor under the number: a five-syllable word. It will have to be written, said, listened to, until it gives way. In the meantime, caution, do not leave it around where it might be seen by just any old so-and-so, friends or others close to you, who are not men: I wouldn't want them to know. Who's playing with me, who shuns me and who cheers me, who gives to me and who takes away from me? Or what does? Is my father a lizard? Or is the lizard my mother's belly? But if it's my mother who ate the lizard, why did she eat it the way Chronos ate his children, by swallowing them headfirst? Unless there was not devouring but rather vomiting: and what I saw during that night so white was not the end of a penetration but a vir-

---

*The French phrase LEZARD. LEVE-TOI! brings to mind its homonymic counterpart, the biblical "Lazare, lève-toi"—"Lazarus, arise"; hence the slightly archaic "arise" has been chosen instead of the more colloquial "get up."—TRANS.

†The letter h in French is pronounced [ȧsh], making it a homonym of hache, or "ax."—TRANS.

ile, bright gray birth. That death was perhaps a birth. So, *am andern Ende,* on the other hand, at this other ending, who's alive? Who's being born down there? Who's dragging in ↓ what?

What?
Arise:
They blew off the rooftops of houses in Santiago, Kleist recounts, so the roofs would not deprive the shut-in virgins of the spectacle outside: the virgin, standing, covered with scars, scarcely clothed in a mourning veil. And the envious virgins confined inside their walls, sticking their heads out through the hole in the roof to see her walk by. Let us suppose that God has a great curved ax [*hache*] and with a broad circular gesture, in one blow, lops off all of that from us. "Hache." My name begins with "Hache." Here's the type-portrait of envious virgins enclosed and rigid inside their walls: they're like the demons of pride, for whom the earth is a pocket of hell. They go about without moving, by means of the powerful contraction of their dorsal and gluteal muscles. Their necks are stiff, their chins set at an obtuse angle to the neck, their eyes, glued to the target, spit, spit, spit, spit. Intense back pain due to the strain of stretching. Their legs dread being flexed. Their necks cannot turn from side to side: they have to rotate their trunks. Their hair is set in ironclad order, curls lined up, cannons loaded. The silence of ecstasy is etched on each line of their faces. Twitching of their feet not afforded a ladder. Favorite daydreams: walking over the faces of all humanity, lying with their backs to the ground, the virgins' feet fitted with shoes that have down-turned, hook-like points. Attending the execution, or better, the public disemboweling, of pregnant virgins who are loved. In silence.

Special peculiarity: they recognize people only after death.

Irises armed with canine teeth. They sleep with their eyes open.

They didn't see anything. Columns were cracking their heads. Their fathers had fallen into the abysses.

★

Who said *Arise?* I did. I heard my voice say "Arise." But it was already a commentary: it was the legend, and as I read it aloud, I was condensing it and I remember being convulsed with laughter. Breaking out, bursting, contractions of knowing amusement that casts me back onto the dividing shore between daytime knowledge and nighttime knowledge. I write, no, I thrust down on a sheet of paper rough-hewn words, the paper takes, the voice dries, the familiar phrase is left. All this is simply a matter of reversal and metonymy: I did not see the mouse, or the lizard, only a tail. From the tail I deduced the animal, as the lizard's belly gave assurance of the back. I could have heard my voice say tail instead of lizard. I'm not used to allusion and substitution. This lizard issues forth from my memory, masculine/feminine, like the Venetian creature, belly and tail, coming out/going in. As a child I lived in a warm climate, in Africa, where the lizard is as common as the earthworm. Since then I've probably seen two or three dart by, by "chance," but they (the lizards) are as far from me as date palms, or as my dead father.

Would I have tried to resuscitate him? But by what name does one summon someone who no longer has ears? It's too late, it has always been too late: from now on he comes when he wants. So it's the man who is not dead I'm calling, as though he were dead, and I give him an order. Arise, I say, and I am the son-daughter of God; I provoke, arise, be object and subject, be father and son, the law and the servant. Stand up, I say, and I am the daughter-wife, I summon you to stop lying down, I raise you up, but it is nevertheless not I who give the order, for at the moment the order is given, the air that I breathe is my mother, and I cut through it with bursts of assertion. "Arise" is said by my voice, but an extra sound slips in with it, a sign that the air I breathe is my mother: wouldn't I have pronounced in a normal situation, *Lizard arise,* following the curve of my voice pattern in an atmosphere entirely my own? Wouldn't I have said, then, *Arise, Lizard!*—avoiding by natural proclivity the solemn apostrophe and thus the metamorphosis of a common noun into a proper noun, of a saurian reptile into a dead man?

It's my mother who urged me forward into this endpoint, *am diesen Ende,* loading down my tongue with the heavy E that knows how to silence itself, the E with the Y, with the EYe that doesn't see anything, with *her* E, the one she begins with, and everything began with Eve.

Hot red lands of Africa, take me into your folds, I am tired, red moving lands mold me in your folds, I want to sleep. That place the lizard stopped is where I lived. The water was blue, thick, and wavy, the tombs on the water's edge were red, my mother spoke a foreign language or else it was they who didn't speak her language, and the paternal language was dead and buried (traces of it remain, but very few) and they spoke a language I didn't know how to write that started on the right and finished on the left, and in which my mother would have been called Ima and my father Baba, but no one was ever named Lazarus on my father's side or in my red lands. No relation, therefore, between Lazarus and me, except precisely this absence of relation, for which reason one could start an argument with me and say there's no tie between

Lazarus and me, that is, that there's the space between his name and mine, without which we'd be confused. For others, Lazarus evokes Christ. That's what I've heard. I know that Lazarus arose. But I don't know where, or how. I know, too, that it's a wonderful event, a celebration of unreason, an accomplished act. Everything carries a weight: perhaps if Lazarus had had a different name, it wouldn't have worked? The air that whispered that sentence to me arose in the east, beyond the deserts, the blue rivers, and the dead seas. But that doesn't mean that I'm prompted by the spirit of the son of God: it's the opposite. My legend did not begin with the order to resuscitate, addressed later to so-and-so. It's the lizard that provoked the cropping up of the sentence, of the part of a syntagma, more precisely the tail end of the formula, to which my mother immediately claimed rights—to tell the truth, my legend is dismembered through analysis: lizard tail + end of formula that splits at the beginning with l → "l'ève" and is weighed down at the center or the belly with an e that's full of itself. One should be able to read: I'm getting up [je me lève], as I used to say playfully to my mother, *Do you love him for me?* in the hopes of getting the love across in double strength, mine and that of the (other).

Hot red lips of T.t., take my tongue into your folds, so that I might get some rest. Hot moving lips, take my tongue and keep it.

I've been talking for hours to T.t. about everything, and we're looking for the lizard. It seems to me that our death took place two thousand years ago, before the Christian era in any case; but the restoration of the world is endless. We make love; the first one who gets up is the other's mother, and so on; to awaken him I call his name through his lips. To put me to sleep he takes me on his lap and, his face tilted toward me, he acts astonished at never having seen me before, because he looks at me with the eyes of an oriental bride-groom. From so much searching, I'm sleepy; I say so to T.t., who says to me: I'm you sleepy. But I try sleeping on his chest, on his stomach, and as I start to doze, I hear him talking, over my waters, it's his voice, air over water, it moves about over the invisible water, spreads over my invisible body a familiar air that rocks me and is very ancient.

> I was placed
> in a large wicker basket
> where they had placed
> my father before me.

But that basket is put away in the dark room with large armoires shut tight, and the room is in my father's mother's house, and my father's mother lives above us, she walks with a heavy step over our heads. To see her, you have to go up one floor in the dark, where the black stairway paneling smells of urine, then knock at the door very loud, kick and pound, the door is gray, enameled with a gray slightly stained with white (black-white gray poorly mixed), my father's mother is the most powerful and the oldest person in the family, she knows French better than my mother and I do, though just barely; for the door to open, you cry: Come in, come in! It's the person on the outside who cries: Come in, Granny! That basket awakens my incredulity: it is so big, what was going on in there?

"Come in, Granny!"
"Who is it?"
"It's me!"

★

This heart is beating in my head: T.t.'s heart has come undone and fallen out of the sky into my cranial cavity by way of my ear, and it bumps and knocks at the top of my head. Little blows of a little hammer, like the doctor's bent index finger as he taps against your chest and listens. Knuckle, a joint—best word in the English language— knuckle, knock, tap-tap-tap, and suckle,* a neighboring word: my ideas revolve around T.t.'s bright heart with a speed at once very great and imperceptible, leaving luminous but ephemeral trails. The heart beats, it's extremely hot, I'm numb, I hardly stir; yes, I hardly stir and my head is glistening, I'm small and long. My head feels heavy because it's so hot, but what is heavy in my head is my tongue, for I think I can move my head, my neck turns on its axis, but the little things, my tongue, my eyelids, even my lips are motionless.

If I weren't sheltered in this hollow alongside Tristan, I'd be afraid. If I were to make a drawing of what I am at this moment, based on what I feel, I'd depict myself as a kind of bird or animal with a narrow body, fairly small, uncommunicative, containing in a membrane (covered with layers of anything, feathers or hairs) a heavy and painful machine that is my real heart, having a fairly long neck, bent but still, and a very beautiful deathly face with the eyes closed and with those anxious, bulging eyelids tightly molded to the eyeball that one sees in that Botticelli painting; this head would not be mine since I don't recognize it, but the head of a bird of prey, nevertheless human. The caption for this image would be the phrase that's giving me so much trouble, and which keeps coming back to crash against my inner mouth as it speaks of itself, and which says: "this phrase is not open enough," as if it meant something else, as if the opening of the phrase, which is the word "phrase" itself, were in fact a blank word, to be replaced by another opening as yet unknown.

*"Knuckle," "knock," and "suckle" are in English in the original.—TRANS.

T.t. is reading the *Gradiva,* I see him reading through the creases of my sleep. I asked him to look for the place where Jensen talks about the lizard for the first time. I start moving around. The pages turn, T.t. reads, the phrase comes back, swirls around, torments me, sticks to the mucous membrane of my throat, chokes me, it's not the first time I've swallowed a fly. I have a violent longing to long to die so that it will come out, but I can't manage to get it started. This phrase is not open enough: through auscultation one locates the dull sounds. T.t. gets excited as he reads on top of me, at times he leans against me and smacks my lips with short, lively, loving kisses, as though I were his daughter. From below I see him, he stretches his neck and smacks my mouth with four kisses. As though he were drinking from my mouth, but drinking what?

★

I recognized my mother by her smile. She was the Beautiful. I wasn't satisfied. I called her. In the process of calling her, I had to name her; from afar, from close by, I called her, my voice was high, it was an order I was giving her, an adoring demand that would not take no for an answer; I had to have that smile:

"Eve, smile!"*

She smiled, I drank it in, I was intoxicated, she turned her head.

"Mama, smile!"

She smiled. "Smile! Smile!" She smiled. "Smile!"

Smile! Beauty! Sunlight!

*The French word *souris,* besides being the second-person imperative of *sourire,* "to smile," also means "mouse."—TRANS.

When we slept together, she didn't smile, I didn't see her smile because she had her back to me. Lying on her side, in a death position, but I was behind her, I protected her, I tightly molded my body into the curve of hers, I hugged her around the waist, I made like a teaspoon. Her stomach was flat and taut with muscles like a nullipara. In the dark she told me stories of when she was little, and I tailored a childhood for myself out of hers, a memory out of hers, and her language in my mouth was German: I talked about things that my eyes had never seen.

Here's what the symbols were of our childhood: snow (a white, creamy coating), skis (a pole with a round thing at the end), all the cousins under the same eiderdown, the river (*die Hase,* the name of a rabbit), the frozen river, the Köln cathedral, the Strasbourg cathedral, the first bicycle (Eve's, because I didn't get one), the forests in springtime, the first storks. My mother's mother, twenty-seven years old, thought that her husband was a pig or an ill-bred Jew (though she knew he was from a good family even if he came from the Austro-Hungarian border) when he wanted to go through the little hole that she used between her legs instead of going through her navel. It was she who in 1915 told my mother how babies came out of cabbages. Her husband was killed that year in Russia by a bullet that took off his legs. This is all part of these *Kinderheitserinnerungen* that served for me as supplementary childhood, as *Urkindheit,* at which, since I know everything, I availed myself of my mother's ignorance. I took from her the river, the snow, the storks. The smile was more recent: in photos from the old days, her lips are turned up like her eyelids, with a neutral, calm mischievousness. That smile is charming and not mysterious. It says: I am exactly what I seem to be. A young virgin desirous of learning. A supple body and wide-open eyes, a bit big. No one ever resembled less an animal. Smile! Eve! Smile!

Revenge of the mouse

T.t dreamed of my dream. Yesterday, while reading the *Gradiva* every which way in search of the lizard, *every which way* he dreams a dream, a dream without a-sin-gle/a dream, where first he sees a mouse come toward the bed; on the bed covered with a thick quilt there is some sort of thing, a thing, some matter, unfamiliar, a what's-it, organic matter not known, and matter he does not want to know. The mouse wants to know, climbs, goes into the thing through a slit; the thing on the bed is cracked, bored through—here I groan in horror, but not T.t.—this is the beginning of the mouse's revenge. What's running, gaping open on the bed, who's feeling and who's suffering and opening up and growing large while the mouse nib-nib-nibbles? Don't find out; what is this mouse? Who's climb-climb-on my bed-climbing? This body on the bed: curdled milk, yes, milky, syrupy liquid that comes from the canal, then curdled, fermented, cut up. *Käse*. *Fromage*-cheese. To smile, say "cheese" and your lips will follow: Tchi:z—*Käse*. Sharp pain then a heaviness in my left arm, from this account. I tell T.t. about what Leonardo da Vinci was playing when he was forty years old: he was playing flying lizard. In Rome, where he had followed Duke Giuliano, he manufactured a wax paste, and while he walked he shaped animals out of it, very delicate, hollow, artful creatures; when he blew inside them, relates Vasari, they flew; when the air went out of them, they fell to the ground. He took this very curious lizard and put wings on it made from the skin of other lizards and then filled the wings with quick-silver, so that they flapped and quivered as soon as the lizard moved; in like manner, he made eyes for this lizard, gave it a beard and horns; he domesticated it, placed it in a box, and used it to startle all his friends.

T.t. tells me that his plowing through the *Gradiva* every which way was in vain, he had to face up to the obvious: the lizard, which first appears in a moving, indistinct group, then isolated and tracked down, is neither green nor gold, but is shiny. Only the knotted blade of grass used to conduct the capture is green. Besides, the lizard is a female, *Lacerta Faglionensis*. It sticks its head out through a jagged cavity before which Zoe-Gradiva's father is waiting, flat on the ground. Zoe's name begins with Z. The lizard watches the old bearded man creep along, it trains its grave, ironic beams on the supine hunter, it is *patient*. Motionless, it smiles. It knows that it can stay nestled in the slit for four hundred years. "This smile is the incarnation of all the amorous experience of civilized humanity." That's what Walter Pater said about the Mona Lisa's smile.

In the same mysterious, terrifying, fascinating manner, Leonardo's winged lizard incarnated the divine experience of humanity: the devilry, the wonders of nature, the father's beard, the body box. A domesticated god took his ingenious body for a walk, and his wings quivered in silence at the slightest move. Leonardo's patience was itself a mad lizard with ineffectual wings, which didn't leave its box through the top because it wasn't aware of its wings. Leonardo painted the way T.t. used to kiss me at times, precipitously, with little repeated pecks, as you kiss quickly and playfully the half-open lips of the lover who's speaking to you. He would get up, dash toward the canvas or the wall, hurl himself forward, and crush the paintbrush here, here, here, here. Then he'd go away for several days or months. Leonardo's lizard has extra eyes and a beard. Is it possible to imagine objects more deserving of disgust than the cheese on T.t.'s bed and this monster with mercury-filled wings? Yet T.t. asserts that he is not filled with disgust but, on the contrary, quite interested. *Käse. Z.** We acknowledge that things have been full of Zs theZe past few dayZ, as though the liZard had laid eggZ all over the place. From that point to saying Sadness. . . . There is *die Mona Lisa,* and *die Marquise von O.*

★

Count F. is a marvelous winged dragon: he takes off into time and space at lightning speed, darting vertically. He is *Impatience.* He snatches life away right in the face, right under the nose, of death. In extremis. He doesn't wait, he doesn't cringe, he doesn't bide his time over the Marquise von O. with courtliness. For he will not put up with any delay. He actuates time, he assumes the strength of ten to jostle existence, he takes the marquise between two fights, embraces her, adores her, impregnates her between two doors, in a hallway, without hurting her, then rushes off to the palace tower, puts out the fires, urgez his soldiers on to action. He'z thought to be seen in a hundred placez at once. There can be no pauze in the implementing of hiz dezires, everything must be seized right away. His power is immediate, absolute, ignited in the blink of an eye, irrezistible. Count F.'s attack and victory supply the figures of Kleist's writing: a word fecundates, one must forever be in a state of ascendancy in order to reach

---

*From this point on in the original, any signifier spelled with an *s* that is sounded *z* is intentionally misspelled with a *z*. Hence the proliferation of similarly misspelled English words.—TRANS.

the place where reazon and natural law cease to be in circulation, where dreams take the form of a female swan named Thinka. Thus the marquise carries in her womb the trace of a unique and fulgurating passage, the mark of that writing that needs not be repeated to be understood.

★

T.t. is handsome. He can be compared to F. in speed and ardor. If I haven't mentioned T.t.'s beauty, it's because I didn't know how to say it. It is essential, in the way I used to think of Eve. He is handsome by the way he surprizez, uplifts, and showz impatience. He'z a supple man, in love with matter, an investigator, continually scrutinizing the lines of bodies, delighted to discover the nearly limitless extensibility of the living, the skin, the imagination, all the cavities of the human body, all the cavities of consciousness, memory, time whoze partitions he has left in abeyance. He'z a man of wonder, of flight. Even Leonardo's lizard pleazes him. He needz to touch, his rough, solid handz have done a lot of touching, trimming, sculpting, painting, caressing. He can actually get bowled over by a vizion: the painting attracts him invincibly, and he leavez behind earth, mother, body, himself and myself, in order to enter it, but he has never failed to come back. Anyway, at theze times his body remains next to me. His childhood iz dead. One can walk over his dead people without giving him a start. However, he waz born of a beautiful, submissive mother whom he brought under his control very early.

The secret of T.t.'s beauty is in the cut of his eyes: it is there that I looked in rapture at peace for the first time. For a long time I sought the secret all over his face, whose asymmetry drew me into long and precious calculations by which I tested the permutations of lines and traits to see where beauty began. I would doubtless never have solved this except by chance. To be sure, I had always associated, in the nonsignifying distance, the curve of his eyelids and the folds of his eyes with his smile: that was normal, his face was totally altered by the broadening of his mouth; what I saw alerted me, so legible was the expression of his eyes, even to a passerby. His eyes declared, fluttered, gently, called. Spoke. "Anybody could understand what your eyes tell me," I warned him, fearing he might be wickedly spied upon. But he smiled, I was taken by him. He coaxes me. He bends forward, he opens his eyes, his eyes fall, they water, running into my eyes: I raise my head. We are motionless—one overall question brackets us:

/this painting is composed in the following manner: I am a cheerful, muscular, plump child, but the shadow that falls over the lower part of my naked body is too dark to be able to tell if I'm a boy or a girl. I'm on the right side of the painting. Here I comment to T.t. that for several weeks I've been living, writing, deciphering, dreaming right to left: everything starts and everything stops me as it comes from the right. I'm trying, it seems, to ride an animal who's bristling (bristle: a word that comes from my mother) and that I hold tight by the ears: it's not a lizard. My right arm is flooded in light. My head is raised, turned from the right side of the painting (my left) toward the left side (my right), and I'm looking for T.t.'s eyes, his forehead being tilted slightly toward me: a straight, almost vertical line can be drawn between point A (top of my head) and point B (top of his head). But now another head comes forward, set back slightly, a long neck emerging from a rounded white breast, scarcely shaded, with a bulging fore-

117

head, full cheeks, nacreous surfaces barely interrupted in their milky swelling by an eye slit, and this full face is as much like T.t.'s as the moon is like the sun, and it interposes itself between the sun and us.

This female figure with pudgy shoulders and adolescent characteristics improperly developed from the albuminous eruption in the skin does not prevent me from seeing T.t.'s head rise up solidly from the superb balancing pole of his shoulders—thus unlike the female double with soft flesh and indistinct features, this female torso that continues down to a body that looks amazingly limp and childlike because of its position (arched back, stomach invisible, gaunt, athletic sagging of the torso toward the knees, thighs spread wide apart wrapped in veils through which the animal whiteness gleams).

T.t. shows his entire face, the features are strong and leave little space for unnecessary surfaces, the oval is delineated vigorously beginning with the chin, and despite the undeniable resemblance to the woman who is interposing, the strength of the nose, eyes, mouth, and chin, the amplitude, as well as the extrusion, of the physiognomy fill me with an exaltation of complicity: in spite of the third person, we are two and we are the victors. Nevertheless, I feel a bit regretful to see that the woman's body is so intrusive: it extends over and even merges with T.t.'s limbs. In fact, she is sitting on him in such a way that one might think she is T.t.'s body. His legs, bent back under the spread veiled thighs, are nearly invisible. At any rate, I can get back the familiar languor of his arms, of his hidden, substituted thighs, because he goes beyond and encompasses this woman from all sides. Their feet are identical, long, white, and solid, used to long walks: that seems to indicate a masculine presence in the young woman there in the flesh— her breasts cannot be seen, moreover, nor where they'd begin, in spite of the extent of flesh left bare from the shoulders down. I might have believed that she was the emanation of his tenderness for me if her face hadn't been engraved with a tenderness even more profound. Anyway, although there's an extra touch of seriousness in T.t.'s look, both he and the woman are of an age that would make the age attributed to me in the composition believable. They both seem to be about thirty. T.t. looks at me and says: how happy I am that you are being born! I attentively follow the phrase that shapes his lips, and it's at that moment that I finally understand the secret of his beauty: I had said, without making of it a decisive observation, that his eyes spoke. In fact, the phenomenon of the eyes' speech is much less simple than that; it has an anatomical cause. Seen from below, the lowered eyelids seem devoid of lashes. They are simply seamed on their outer border with a shadow that thickens them in such a way that they seem to be half-open lips. Whence the strange emotion that stabs me with each of his looks: these lips have the intense and innocent look of mystical ignorance. Drinking and seeing blend there where they open, these eyes kiss my eyes and my lips, they touch, taste, take. The look of mystical ignorance is that which responds best to all demands and all needs, for it never refuses anything. Good nurturing eye.

Lips of T.t., look at me, nurturing lips open up. Tristan, lip us up.*

When he came back to me across the blue waters and the red waters, T.t. had opened those original eyes whose color was that opaque, murky, milky blue that only suckling infants' eyes have. This blue of primal ignorance colors the

---

*In the French, *lèvres* is a neologism that turns *levres,* "lips," into a second-person imperative, through its graphic similarity with *lève,* "lift" or "arise" (see note on page 104).—TRANS.

sole cloak that girds the double mother represented by Leonardo in the figures of Anne with eyes resembling oracular lips and of Mary with eyes resembling the mouth of a timid lover. T.t.'s lips as he leans over me have a slight smell of colostrum.

There is the painting, with three of us in it, and in which no one yet knows what I shall be, except what T.t. announces to me: you will be born. Then, there are all those photos that were taken thirty years ago in which there are two of us, my father and I. Where was my father's wife when I was born? Based on the photos and my memories, it is obvious to T.t. that *I am my father's daughter.* T.t. is perfect. T.t. is not dead. T.t. is not my father. What's more, I forbid him to die.

I am sitting on his lap in the position of the painter's mistress, and we're looking at this painting that he explains to me, then at these photos, his, then mine. In his, you see his mother: he's two years old, in the middle distance, sitting on sand. The rectangle is divided into two triangles, one is made up of the sand, the one on the left, the other is entirely taken up by his mother, who blocks the sky as she stoops over him, a large, beautiful, motionless lizard, with her hair falling down, arched over her little boy. As beautiful as it may be, this writing with light, imbued with maternal love, the blocked triangle gives the impression that the darkness is going to fall into the white sand and envelop the little boy with its hair. The arch of the dark flesh bewitches him, mesmerizes him. Come, say the black lips, come on, get up! Here's my mother when I was little. She is alone on the beach, the sand forms a warm couch for her, she is parallel to the sky; it's Eve, she's smiling, her even teeth shine, her steady eyes shine, her eyelids are lifted high. She is a young girl, virgin and pregnant, without a trace of the labors of childbirth. Warm flesh, chestnut hair; she's a princess. She has come to this country because it's exotic, but it's her snow that melts the sun.

She is looking at us. My father and I are crouching in symmetrical positions on the sand, in front of her. In the photo I'm on the right. I frown and attack; this shadow will have to be covered with sand. I am my father's daughter. In this photo here it's even clearer: he's standing up to his full height, without feet because he takes up too much space. There are two of us, that's too many. I am lifted up high, he's raising me, his left arm holds me round my thighs, I aim for his jacket pocket, and I hang onto him as I wriggle, trying to go into the pocket by slipping my feet in first. It's good to be in your father's pocket. I frown and say: I want to.

I still hear the thunder back then, thirty years ago, the corrective voice of my father's powerful mother.

"We don't say I want to, we say I would like to."

Wherein she's mistaken, for it's precisely *I want* that you should say.

★

The mother whose breast Leonardo is sucking is metamorphosed into a vulture that puts its tail into the mouth of the infant in the cradle. Then the vulture that asked for the infant's mouth is metamorphosed into a blue cloak that girds the double mother of the painting.

Moses, out of the cradle, crawls forward as far as the fire pit and brings an ember to his mouth: because of this event, his burnt tongue will fail him; but, I said to my mother, how could he bring the ember to his mouth without burning his hand?

There have been many other enigmas since I started reflecting on such tales. It was Eve who told them to me: her stories always began with *when*.

★

With his tiny handwriting that leaned from right to left, Leonardo took notes intended just for himself. He said "tu" to himself: he gave himself orders. Who needs a father?

★

He said "tu" to himself: "Learn the multiplication of roots from Master Luca."

By saying "tu" to himself, he multiplied himself by two. If I were to say "tu" to myself, I'd be the lizard. And what if the lizard were me? I say to T.t., what if it weren't you I forbade to die, and what if I were the one who gave the order and the one who received it? This phrase is not open enough! Listen: and if "Lizard, arise" is said by the voice I have for speaking to myself, then I am the son of God, I am dead, I return from the dead, I am "you" and I am you T.t., whom I caress so that afterward you'll be my father and my mother. But not God.

Leonardo says "tu" to himself in the imperative; he's a master.

T.t.! I say. I'm sitting on his lap, I kiss his breast, which I wouldn't take for the maternal teat. I interrupt myself to say his name in an urgent manner: T . . . t . . . ! Yes. T.t.! Yes. For certain parts of his body I feel a love in my eyes and in my tongue, which is not only physical, but also, especially, spiritual. I have a spiritual need for his chest. While my tongue recognizes that slight, strange, acrid taste where he dissolves, my eyes follow the tense, muscular curve of a torso that, seen from here where I'm nestled, resembles the earth's outer crust reproduced in books to demonstrate that the planet is round: on the horizon a truncated boat, a caravel. It is round. His chest is thus my earth and my horizon. My soul loves his chest. Inside and out. I'm not getting mixed up, I'm not looking for his breast. If that were what I was looking for, I'd go to my father's elder sister, my food-aunt, my resting-place, my maternal cushion. What my soul wants from T.t. is his heart and his lungs, and that's the horizon.

We know all that. And also that life is at times staked on a phrase, or even a single sign, which could be perhaps a folded sentence, or even a single letter on which the whole thing hinges. Thus, who will ever be able to measure the effect of the following phrase that Eve heard her mother repeat at a time when she still had never seen the sea, and when the Orient was keeper of the fruits: *Kennst du das Land wo die Zitronen blühen,* and the aggravating yet delicious effect on my ear, from childhood on, of the z (ts) sound made by the "tsitrus" words? So with lizard. I am prey to phrases. For how many days have we been on the road? For several weeks, an uncertain number of months, we've been in a state of renewed commotion. According to the sky, which we both take a look at with a single movement, it's impossible to decide the month of the year. According to T.t.'s watch, it's December, but the sky sows the colorful signs of May. So it's been several weeks and several months since we started, and yet T.t.'s watch is a flawless instrument. We've got to accept, then, that this December is our May, which is no contradiction to us. It's not surprising, with time having this extensibility, that I should often experience physical exhaustion, accompanied by a fever, uncontrollable movements, a sensation of dizzying exaltation, and always this slight, strange, spinning gravidity, as if: "I'm losing my balance," "things are on the decline and turning me upside down," "I live from right to left." Let's give birth to it, says T.t.

And here we are auscultating the belly of the phrase to see if it has reached term.

He says: Get up [*Lève-toi*]. Then: lift, Eve, lift, calf, bear, veld [*L'ève, l'ève, l'ève, vèle, vèle, vel*].

I: Live, vile, vile, There's the I that has come out. Live, levi, levite, avoiding it [*l'évite*].

He: Tail, life. Life, die! death, die!

Whose tail? Tail: exact length of the question. Q *is* a question. It appears to me that the letter Z has become at once the sign of the lizard, of Being, of the Letter, and the concrete frame, as a bedframe, in direct proportion to the question. Can you tail me what arise [*lève-toi*] means, levi, levite, the code falls apart very quickly now, I say lizard, then my tongue says Caesar, then we talk about the *Käse* on T.t.'s bed, and about that perforating mouse, and about Kleist's Swansign [*Sygne*] named Thinka, who divided the waters with fire. Where are we going with such speed? Where we won't lose our balance anymore. Now I'll tell Thot about the marvelous maneuver by which the Marquise von O. became the Count of O.

★

The Marquise von O. loses her balance for the first time, the night of the siege, when Count F., like an angel from heaven, having grabbed her from the pack of wanton dogs and then courteously conducted her to a wing of the palace still intact, speaks to her in French. The second time, after Count F. has disappeared, is when, during a medical examination, in the course of which the midwife keeps on talking, as she looks her over, about blood, youth, and people's wicked tongues, the Marquise von O. thinks she's losing her mind; here's the tenor of the matron's talk: that the hearty corsair who landed on the island of her widowhood for a night of love "would surely be found in the end"; that besides the Holy Virgin no woman on earth had ever had this happen to her.

The marquise desired the earth to open to make way for her. Not so much to stay there, but to seek refuge close by the angelic F., of whose recent death she was aware. If she had conceived without being holy or a virgin, and without being governed by natural law, then nothing was impossible anymore. The marquise drew herself up to the full height of a body stretched by pride and astonishment, so that she was taller than her own father. Because of her decision to go beyond, without tripping, the laws of the earth and of reason, she was in metamorphosis: she could henceforth deny her heaviness if necessary. She could no longer be hemmed in by the horizontal world. Were it not a child filling her without heaviness, nothing would have put the brakes on her assumption. Because of the child, she ascended slowly, head-first, and her flight was like that of a swimmer, the body contracted by the effort. She pulled up and pushed out each limb in turn, opening and closing a figure Z in space. In the end her vertical soul would fly up among the angels, as the Count d'Orgaz's soul can be seen to ascend from the horizontal plane of Toledo where his burial is taking place, across a cloudy gorge, with the lightness of one of Leonardo's birds filled with air.

Because she believed in the soul, and since she also believed in the laws of the body and the ways of conception, the Marquise von O. wasn't afraid. She could very well put her life back into motion, with O. as her base, as she had done when she'd just lost her husband. She didn't deny feeling a strange joy at this new beginning that cut her off from the earth and from the tomb, so she looked toward the delivery as the occasion for her own birth in a new place.

At the height of this spiritual mutation that put her on the same rung as birds and angels, her emotion was so great (at times even to the point of being amorously transported by herself, taking on the appearance of Count F. and just for fun naming herself the Count von O.) that she went ahead and knitted little bonnets and stockings for little legs.

Do you know, T.t., what the Marquise von O.'s venerable mother calls her daughter when she is convinced of her "innocence"? She calls her "magnificent and superhuman creature," and "my little dear." These are the words used by the venerable and feisty mother when her daughter, widowed and pregnant, gets up, taller than her own father, having gone beyond the limits separating the human and the divine.

One after the other, the Marquise von O., Governor G., Lady G., Count F., the Marquise von O., Governor G., Lady G., Count F., Governor G., Count F., fall to their knees and ask: "Do you still love me?" The Marquise von O. helps the governor and her mother to their feet. To the count she just says: stand up.

In the end Governor G. takes the pregnant Marquise von O. on his lap, he places on her mouth long fiery kisses, he sheds on her lips bright tears, he pats the belly where everything is making ready. He is happy, though he doesn't say so, that this child has no father. No other father. He caresses with his fingers and lips his daughter's mouth, and he places on her wondrous belly long earnest kisses.

In time, the familial and amorous functions are transformed. Outside of time sometimes as well. If it weren't for the order of procreation, we could see more clearly: we could bring into play new classifications, we could produce new systems, which would be at times surprising to those who loathe the transformational combination (however necessary) and who prefer to believe that original structures are sacred and fixed. How to explain the difference in behaviors and functions of set E between the initial time O and time B except by putting the primitive system back into operation. Things *are* this way, if only we could refrain from relying on that crutch "as if." Governor G. is his daughter's bewildered lover. Lady G. is the grandmother of her husband, the governor. The Marquise von O. is her father's young mother. Count F. is an angel. He is a demon from hell. He is an angel come from heaven. The Marquise von O.'s brother is a forest ranger. He's a cretin, a messenger. The Marquise von O. is the youthful, ardent father of her two little children who are not separated from her and who don't have first names.

La Gradiva is the ideal housewife, an indulgent woman to her absentminded men, her father's nourisher. Old Bertgang is an animal savant. Jensen says that young Norbert Hanold is for the Gradiva an archaeopteryx. Gradiva-Zoe owns a cage with a singing canary inside, in the window of her house in Germany. Josephine and Jeronimo precede and surpass all structures. They have nothing to do here or there.

My mother is a young virgin princess who smiles at me. She is primordial. T.t. is not my father. I had a father in the past, the father of my childhood. My other fathers are all dead and forgotten. T.t. is my accomplice. He's well-built; when I'm tired of searching, I fall asleep, he takes over for me. His body can also be the delegate of my body. At times I'm one year old, and he teaches me to walk. At times he is born, and I teach him to see.

My father is a bird. T.t. says I'm my father's daughter. Eve gives him to me willingly; she says "Your father." He taught me words, Eve taught me sentences. He judged and he punished; between the sentence and the execution a little time went by. He was also a sorcerer, he cured, he chastised, he gave orders. He put on a white hat, a "Panama," a helmet, a kepi, a brushed felt scout's cap. He was handsome, he frequented high places, he led troops of boys who called him Stork. He glided and he traveled, lanky, fragile, heavy and light—this is not a contradiction. My father takes me in his beak. It doesn't hurt. I am what he found.

Here I catch my breath before going still faster toward the discovery of the Supreme Cause (sz), I am in between what I've said and what I'm going to say.

Between [*Entre*] is T.t. Enter [*Entrez*] is me.

I've caught the thread that reels out the intertwined strands that fill my memory to perfection, I have my whole life to wind it in; it's really necessary for me to take time off sometimes, to catch my breath in the silence, while T.t. holds the thread for me.

Only the sun does not move. Things go fast, the story has picked up a lot of speed. Phrases follow one another now too fast to have the time to ripen. They burst open as they come to me and inundate me; they fall on me from above, they pester me with pecks of their beaks. The beaks are aquiline or long and straight, hard fingers of God, flying penises, pen, pain, penalize. They are heavier and heavier, short but packed. And above all they must be written: I need to catch my breath because of this heavy writing that I transmit from top to bottom and from right to left, in this little tiny hand (in English you can suppress the second part of the word "handwriting"; you can say he has a lovely hand. In German, too, you write with the hand, yet in French no hand is mentioned), this condensed writing, infinitely powerful but not voluminous, which surpasses me and drags me along by its own weight, more ponderous than mine.

Since the beginning of this story, the frequency of contradictions has been increasing. Scarcely am I touched by T.t. when a phrase arrives. Here's one that takes hold of me while I'm sitting on his lap and is written right after his question: "Do you know where we are?" In terms of what he desires and according to the painting, I could have answered: "in our eternity," or "out in the country, a place I don't know, on the horizon of which strange, narrow, volcanic basins are broken into vertical valleys," or else, as part of this infinite circulation in which we've been engaged since we started to cease dying, I could have said with good reason, "in Pompeii, in Santiago, in each other's arms, at the origin, *am andern Ende,* at the end, which end? and even over there where the cracks in the earth are red and gold, in Tipasa, dead town from my second childhood in Spain, in Germany, in Palestine, at the intersection, in the Orient, on the edge of the Mediterranean basin, in our bed, on our land." But a phrase is written which, as soon as I've heard it in all conscious innocence, astonishes me, turns against me, vicious and beautiful, strikes me violently, on the ears, in the neck, on the lips, twists, a reptile of brute force—and yet—beautiful: "the nearby is far away." It's not the contradiction that makes me choke. I've known about the Nearby—the marriage of heaven and hell—for a long time. It's the sound of this phrase, which has the oracular, curt, and open voice that speaks to me in my first dreams of the night; a voice without timbre, so clear that it's always impossible for me to tell who's speaking, man, woman, god, or myself, so succinct and right that a laugh of discovery wells up in me. However, the phrase is given to me in the dark: I don't understand it, which doesn't prevent me from knowing unhesitatingly that it shows me everything. The-nearby-is-far-away has that quality of a nocturnal lightning flash that the lizard had, the only difference being that the lightning is washed out in the sunlight. This phrase knows not what it says.

That's why the phrase remains immobile at first in dazzled sleep!

Il sole non si muove.

In the end it is I who move. I roll it around in my mouth, I embody it, I turn it over very quickly in every direction. Its body was so impersonal that at first it moved me very little: the nearby is no one and belongs to no one. If they'd wanted to throw me off the track of the secret without a scandal, they could have chosen a cleverer formulation. For the nearby doesn't interest me—distance, or its variations, I'm indifferent to—not as a singular subject, or as a universal subject, or as a substance or concrete term. And besides, this distance not traveled and yet unfurled between here and there puts me off. The phrase is pendulous. Doesn't affect me at first—then:

Something extraordinary happens:

The moment I think the phrase is gone—and I don't hear it anymore, I don't listen to it anymore, it must have swung off down there at a tangent from heaven to earth, I thought: it gets me at ground zero (where, under my closed eyelids, the bulging ocular globes resemble little eggs under the membrane) where I neither think nor foresee—and makes me fly off in a flash. Crater. Whence rises, a root in the air, the tree of recognition. Another mouth has opened up to me in the center. What does it say?

It says: "I am behind." So be it.

Inside I saw the river of the night flow into the river of the day and yet their waters did not merge. Then I saw Kleist's white bird, I called it by name, for I didn't know the feminine form of the word "swan"; I said Thinka in a very high singing voice, and it paddled forward, its immensely long, thin, graceful neck on the border between the waters of the night and the waters of the day, and it was the line of its passage that separated the waters. I said: Thinka, I desired it, I wanted it to lay its neck down against me, and I would have slipped my long slender arms around the base of its neck. It was swimming on this section of water that I saw flowing between the mouth of the rivers and the horizon in order to show me something: the movement of its body was designed for me, aimed at me; I understood: I am the straight line. The waters, drying out behind it, were covered with dust, red lands (from that I deduced: white + black = red; in other words: day + night = blood). These sets summoned up, as an echo, the striking phrase: I imagined a result sprung from contradictory forces, which was red-life.

Thinka, cutting through the water, changed to the color of blood before my eyes. It was red, dripping with black water and white water.

The mouth in the center said: the Occident is the Orient.

I didn't care. On the other hand, what happened to the bird impressed me: once out of the water, its red body with the immensely thin red neck tingled, sending out sparks. As in a dream, I felt my own flesh tingle, sweat. My soul, having taken refuge as far from the surface as possible, was clouded in mourning, and I kept suffering and seeping until the mouth said to me: "You are last. Pass to the other side." To my astonishment, the mouth spoke to me in a foreign language that I recognized right off while also being grieved to hear it and recognize it. I tried to plug my ears.

Listen, I say to T.t., I'm being spoken to from somewhere else, very far from here, so I can't hear you. It wasn't the first time I heard this language spoken that I didn't recognize. It was spoken in the streets of my first childhood, over my head and at some distance from my body. I set my back against the red letter-box with red letters, which wants to spit up a memory against me.

"Listen," I say to T.t., "ever since you asked me: 'do you know where we are?' I no longer know where I am, things are constantly in movement, no matter what I do, I'm sitting on your lap and yet I've crossed over centuries, I travel, a voice without timbre leads me, which is perhaps my voice from somewhere else or from the depths.

"Listen," I say, "it told me that the Occident is the Orient. I am here, I see you, I see your eyes seeing me: and everything I see is red, I see red everywhere, what is it?"

One must always say what one doesn't know. The pure air cracks open the phrases to pluck from them the still-living fruit. T.t.'s tongue can even go looking in my mouth for the phrase that comes out wrong. T.t. probes: where does the red come from? What's the exact shade of that red? Is it blood red, purple, scarlet, carmine?

That depends. It's a deep lively red, at times as though it were seen through a fine film of amber.

Here are the languages to which I was apprenticed in my first childhood, because my father willed it: first Arabic, then Hebrew, later Chinese.

I do not speak any of those languages. I no longer know

how to write them; I suffered through the apprenticeship the way you suffer through physical therapy: the exhausting gymnastics are vain, you'll never walk, you'll never talk. I learned powerlessness.

After his death I learned other languages that I know how to speak. For a long time I thought that my father's languages had missed the mark with me because they came from too far away. They were Oriental. What's left of them? Letters, two alphabets, a few words held in escrow.

When you express the idea that the other person has a mysterious language, which isn't sinking in at all as you listen, you say: it's Greek to me; or else: it's Chinese. But you don't say: it's Arabic.

When the young Norbert Hanold wanted to speak to the Rediviva girl, his heart almost stopped beating: which language should be used to question a young Pompeian who died two thousand years before and has come back? A dead language or a modern one?

He wants to ask her who she is, here, now that she's come back.

The Gradiva is sitting in the sun between two yellow columns, halfway between the shafts. She doesn't move. But inside her body resides movement. Her dress with the numerous folds is yellow. The archaeologist speaks to her first in Greek, in case she's the daughter of the poet Meleager, then in Latin, in case she's the prettiest girl of Pompeii. The Gradiva answers him in German. Her voice is clear, deep, heavy; it leaves traces of bronze in the air. My voice is high. T.t.'s voice is sometimes deep and full, sometimes high and resonant. Eve's voice is deep and calm. Very calm and distant. It's a perfect voice for telling stories: there's already an elsewhere in its timbre before she has pronounced the first words that carry me off. I have never been: in Italy, in Greece, in Palestine, in the Orient. But I can imagine them. The images are in color, are color. I see Italy, Greece, Palestine, the Orient without cities, without monuments, without streets, without noise other than the vague general hum of presence. I see their great elemental bodies, their drowsy, twitching flesh, their extremities, saltwater lips, the heat of their lands massed together at noon in the sun; I see all that in large thick colored segments in movement, in respiration. They are mothers, elemental, animal, mute, welcoming. I have a desire to sleep there.

Because of saying no, the "no" becomes exhausted. When it falls, dead skin, it's surprising to see the dazzling yes that the dry flower scarcely camouflages anymore; it's not surprising, for the yes is hardly seen before you admit that you've always heard it under the no, that you've simply delayed the time of the fruit, to swell the in-between time when things are going to be and aren't. The admission is a pleasure. It's natural to save the fruit for dessert. The best fruits are those that are bitten into, divided, multiplied, made to last. Pomegranates, for example, produce by their multiple composition a kind of refined, distant pleasure; by their color, too, a deep red, at times lighter, by the white pit, visible transparently, lodged at the heart of each seed, by the extreme thinness of the golden-yellow membranes that partition the sections of fruit, by the crown with pointed teeth that protect their external sex organ, by their thick skin, a fragrant red and greenish-yellow hide that encloses it. What is more, ripe pomegranates split open by themselves under the sun. The yeses of scarlet glass can then be seen between their lips.

What prevented me from wishing to admit that I knew

the language spoken around me? It's what prevented me from placing "The nearby is far away" opposite "Lizard, arise." That's the reason, since I resisted, that there was red everywhere: that red is the blood of my memory. My memory is a placenta. It's the red land that nourishes my future. As for the tree that grows with its root in the air, one need only turn it upside down for it, with its head up, to reveal what it is by its fruit. It's the pomegranate tree from the night in Chile, which filtered the moonlight and sheltered the trinity wrapped in a blue cloak. It's the upright tree of disavowal, the one that makes men believe that paradise sprouts up in the midst of men and that innocence is headquartered at equal distance from the Temple pillars.

There is no trace of a green lizard in the *Gradiva*. Green is the color of the clip that held the cloak of the lover hidden in the arms of her lover two thousand years ago. But there is a red sea that covered over the dead paving stones and the faded mosaics. This sea is not a sea: it's an immense field of red poppies, sprouted from the combination of natural forces and immortal seeds. Jensen says that this field was motionless, hypnotized, real. The movement is illusory: it's the motionless movement of a color outspread under the sun; the light disturbs what's before our very eyes, that which nothing can make move.

All this is in reference to red and to the sea, to the fruits of the pomegranate tree, to Eve's voice, to the strong May sunshine (for it is May) on the flowers, to the yellow pillars of Pompeii, to the pillars of day and of night that preceded the Hebrews in the desert that extends between Egypt and Canaan, to the parting of the waters of the Red Sea before the children's steps, as they crossed the dry bed between two walls of red water, to the double pillar of God which separates those who speak Hebrew from those who speak Pharaoh's language and which was night for the latter and for the former a light in the night. And it was the same pillar, and regardless of how close the former were to the latter they were nonetheless infinitely far apart. Because they didn't see one another.

It is I, Moses, and I lift a rod, and the red waters rise up to my right and to my left, and they stay that way.

T.t. and I go across. Our feet at the same time on the same sand, at noon. Eve is no longer here. She is behind us. When it surges back to cover the army, the chariots, the men, the horses, the king, the force of the sea is irresistible. In Hebrew the word for sea is masculine.

The immobile sun mobilizes the colors and brings the red to life.

God speaks to Moses. It is not said in which language, but it's a safe bet that He speaks to Moses in his fathers' language.

The language that I didn't want to know anything about is not my fathers' language, nor my mother's. Imagine if God had spoken to Moses in Egyptian. Wouldn't Moses have choked? Wouldn't he have hesitated and even refused to cross the Red Sea, even if God had told him that on the other shore everything would be translated?

The language that made me hesitate is Arabic. In this language father is said Baba. Door is Bab. What's it doing here in my ears, this language that speaks against me, unless it's here to deafen me? That's why I wanted to plug my ears. Thus I kept at a distance the proximate dangers. We close our eyes, we plug our ears, we turn our backs to a double-sided pillar: then we don't risk seeing the blackness gape before us or hearing the hinges squeak or seeing the yes issue forth from the no.

Lazarus is not for me. It's my willful fault if that phrase is not open enough: I didn't want its openness. I felt like stopping there, placing my head on the step of the Temple of Apollo, not giving birth, going to sleep, on the edge of the Mediterranean basin, without ever crossing it, before the beginning of the story, wrapped in the innumerable folds of a dress that would be neither green nor red nor blue.

Finally the red sea opens and rises up.

"The nearby is far away" is my rod: I lift my words, and the phrase opens up into two symmetrical walls, united and separated by the faraway-nearby. On the right the voice commands: Lizard, arise! On the left the voice commands: Open sesame!

Who says this phrase in a high loud voice?

It's Ali-Baba, standing, trembling, before the door of the cavern. This door (Bab) was so small and so well hidden by bushes that Ali-Baba, who thought he knew the mountain in which the door had been cut, never saw it. It's my mother who told me that marvelous Oriental tale, making her voice resonate with bronze tones, in the past, when I adored her, at the time of Smile.

She says: Open sesame! So then at the foot of the mountain the door opens wide to let Ali-Baba in.

What do the Gradiva and Ali-Baba have in common? The I and the A. What do the marquise, Moses, you-T.t. [*T.oi.t.*], Jeronimo, and Josephine have in common? The O.

What do sesame and the lizard have in common? The Z, the S, the A.

What do Occident and Orient have in common? The pillar of god. The daynight.

For a long time I'd known all that without seeing it.

Why, if I knew it, did it take me so many days to see it,

why did I cross so many deserts, centuries, beds of sand, beds of ashes, why did I translate so many narratives, why did I divert so many waterways and raise so many walls, block so many roads, why did I try to have the sun rise at sunset?

—It can be seen by that that I want to gain time—

Because I was afraid that black might be white, that my mother might be my father, that my father might be my mother. That my paternal language might slip, that my forked tongue might put a siren in my mouth.

Amidst the divided waters Thinka has become red. To pronounce this name you have to first place the tip of your tongue between your teeth. Thinka's neck is immense; it is larger than that of an ordinary swan. One might say it's a stork's neck. At the end of its journey when all the waters have become red lands behind it, Thinka falls asleep. Sleep rises, arrives on the eastern shore of the Mediterranean basin, and digs a hole. Then sleep lays a white egg inside awakening. Out of it will come a nightmare.

When I said: Lizard, arise! I was the son of God and I was rising.

When I say Open sesame! who am I? I am Ali-Baba, I want to go deep into the mountain by the secret door. If I steal from the thieves, I'm not a thief. Thieves don't steal in any case in our region. It's carefree young men who steal things elsewhere and conceal them here. They rob down there and hide their loot here.

Lizard-arise was the column of clouds that separated me from Open-sesame. Sesame was too close to me to be too far away. What is so close that it can only be seen as something far away? The man when he wants to catch hold of the woman and, passing his hands over her, no longer sees himself and no longer sees her. The invisible child in his mother's womb. Here I would need music to represent the proximity of death, which is the very movement of life: death is that rhythmic heaviness that forces us to return to the ground and even to plunge into it in order to get over the efforts required by the dance of life. Death is in the womb of life. It kills us when it is born. Unfortunately, I am wanting in the arts. Fortunately, Sesame iz not far off.

I say: Open sesame! because I want to know what there is on the other side of the door. It is clear that I'm playing at making love to the mountain. The mountain rises up. Words are what open it. Eve told me how Ali-Baba's wicked older brother, who was rich and jealous, forgot the formula, so shaken had he been by the emotion of seeing the riches. He would have liked to stay with the gold for eternity. But he was afraid of the stalwart thieves. That's the way Sesame disappeared. So: he tries all the cereals and all the grains—corn, wheat, barley, oats. Ali-Baba expected to enter into a narrow, dark cavern, but he finds himself in a high, bright vault, built on raised columns, whose brilliance comes from the glitter of piles of gold and silver. An interior temple. Gold is on the inside.

Now then, I'll stop being Ali-Baba, for I don't want to carry off the gold.

T.t. tells me that, though he hasn't found the green lizard, at least he's found the red butterfly that lands on the Gradiva's hair just at the moment when Norbert is speaking to her in Greek, then in Latin, then in German. This butterfly has golden wings edged with a fine red border. It's a cleopatra. At the second encounter, during which the archaeologist draws near the girl, a fly lands on the Gradiva's delicate hand. The long hand with supple, slender fingers. The archaeologist is consumed with a ferocious desire to touch her in order to verify:

if the hand is alive, it follows that the whole body is alive. He could touch her hand with his, he could press his lips against it, he could rub it, take it, but his hand offers resistance: impossible to lift it; there's no use admonishing it, the weight of his hand has become immense. It is pinned to the stone on which he had placed it, or maybe it's glued, or petrified. How hateful yet enviable is that fly!

The cleopatra butterfly, which seems born of the contact between the red sea and the sun, judging from the color of its wings, is an imaginary creature. There is a strange mechanism that plays with time: it's because N. H. believes for an instant, the instant of the question in Greek, that the Gradiva is the daughter of the poet Meleager, that the cleopatra lands on the brown hair of Cleopatra. Cleopatra killed herself upon learning of her husband's death. I'd kill myself, too. The butterfly is thus born of the archaeologist's ephemeral illusion. Here it's not clear anymore where things are coming from and where they're heading. The fly was perhaps born of the harrowing need to verify that haunted Norbert. If the nearby is far away, the faraway can also be near and desire can bring forth its reality.

My mother had the habit, at the time she told the tale of Ali-Baba, of pronouncing familiar and compelling maxims. She said: Heaven helps those who help themselves. I helped myself. T.t., who is me, helps me. One can help oneself infinitely, the power having no limit except for when one departs for the divine. All tools are good, be they ephemeral or not, human or not. They increase the chances. When Moses had to confront Amalek's army, he divided up his forces in the following manner: he said to Joshua, choose your men for us, go out, do battle with Amalek. And I shall go to the mountaintop with the rod of God in my hand. Here are the tools that

Moses uses for the war against Amalek. He uses: the strength of men, the authority of the leader of his army, the mountaintop, the rod of God. He's helping himself. At the end of the rod he's holding in his hand above the battlefield there is divine power. But the hand is the locus of human power, for god, who has a right and a left since he created the world, has no hand. By dint of keeping his arms raised up over the bloody plain, Moses felt a great muscular strain and his hands became heavier than hands of stone. He could have summoned god to aid him. But the son should not turn to his father so long as he can subject nature to his desire. Here's how Moses remains the victorious son: he downsizes. The son is the master of the Number and there's only one god. Moses has recourse to two extensions: Aaron and Hur each hold up one of his hands, one on one side, the other on the other side. With three, Moses holds out, and his hands do not budge until the sun goes down.

The fly holds up Hanold's heavy hand: through a system of organic magnetism; its tiny gyration galvanizes his nerves, which then makes this weighty mass rise to the rigid joints from the shoulder to the elbow, from the elbow to the wrist. His arm rises. An instant later his palm crashes down on the long hand with supple fingers. It is not known what becomes of the sacrificial fly.

★

When the Red Sea opens to allow the Hebrews to pass, it is at full dilation. When it returns to its regular form and closes it is in the masculine. It's still the Red Sea. When Ali-Baba cries out *Open sesame,* the door opens wide, when he cries *Close sesame,* the door closes back up and the mountain is impregnable. It's the same mountain, hollow, full, opening, and closed.

In the cavern, sacks of gold, sacks of silver. Asses, mules, horses, asses. Thirty-eight men in thirty-eight goatskin bottles with just a narrow slit for air. Thirty-eight daggers. A man cut up and quartered then sown back together by hand. Little sloping streets. A woman who sees everything. The sign of lamb's blood on the crossbeam and on the two doorposts, the night of Passover. Sign of the white X on the door and on all the doors of the little street, then sign of the red X on the door and on all the doors of the little street where Ali-Baba lives. During the night Ali-Baba and Morgiane bury thirty-eight stalwart thieves in a row in a flower bed of loose soil. Then they tamp the soil down.

★

In order for the gray door pierced with a tiny peephole to open for me, I had to cry: Come in, Granny! as if it were she who wanted to enter where I am outside, whereas I want to get inside, into my father's mother's house. I wanted to enter into the vestibule, then into the black bedroom where my father came from. For I am my father's daughter. In the bedroom there were black lacquered armoires decorated with fine gold bas-reliefs. Golden storks twisted their necks amidst reeds that raised their gold-hooded heads around a vertical basin of oval glass in which one could see one's reflection. This still water absorbed the light in which I was bathed. In the black armoire, beyond the still water, there is the book of birds that no one has ever read. (Tristan says that I look more and more like this bird.) There are birds that go up, birds that go down, and birds that dive. It is written that birds have knowledge of time, and that men are ignorant of time. Jeremiah says that if men do not know it's time to rise up, there will befall them a time of calamity: the bones of kings and the bones of princes and the bones of priests and the bones of prophets and the bones of men will be spread out under the eyes of the sun, and of the moon, and of the stars that will gather them back together and will not raise them, and the bones will be excrement spread across the face of the earth; because men will not have known how to live, or how to know. While the dove and the swallow and the stork keep watch over the time of their coming, "*turtur, et hirundo, et cyconia custodierurunt tempus adventus sui.*"

My father is dead. He was a stork. He knew when he had to live and when came the time to die. My mother is a mouse. She loves life about which she has a great curiosity; she runs all over the place. She's always forgetting her watch. Heinrich Cornelius Agrippa says in *De occulta Philosophia, sive de Magia* that birds have a premonitory sense. *Cyconia, concordiae avis, concordiam facit.* That is true. My father: *altivolans.* He flew high. He desired at a high level as well. It's from him that I get my ardent desire for great heights. *Cyconia advena:* that's a migratory, messenger bird. Things happen quickly, on high. There are birds that descend, like the vulture who is said to be always female, there are birds that dive down, like the swan.

★

Bird [Oiseau]: the first riddle that my father, who was master of words and of letters, asked me, when I reached the age of reason. He lifted me up high onto his shoulders, he put me on the ground. For the right to have another ride to the sublime, I had to answer this question: "What contains all the vowels and is split by a consonant with a double meaning?" I was standing in front of him, and people were whispering to me all sorts of words, and my tongue was racked with fear in my mouth, as if it wanted to flee; my legs gave way, my father lay down and stretched out, I lifted my eyes toward his eyes and the sunlight plunging into my tears blinded me; I saw my father's face now only far off, and so high that its vague, scintillating contours blurred together with the sunlight, his hair blazed red, my father's head was solar and motionless, it must have enucleated the sun and become lodged in its core, or else the sun had come unhooked by itself—in any case: the sky around the flaming head with the invisible face was black; a ball of fire hit my chest and went through me without killing me; nonetheless, I thought I was going to die, or rather I wanted to die, but I didn't know how to die, which way to die, I knew only that I exulted and I despaired, that I had just figured out what I would henceforth want until old age, I knew the meaning of the word "die," which I had never yet used; dying was the opposite of chance. It was wanting. And wanting was the opposite of chance. It was adoring. And it was possible to adore. And adoration is death. I dawdled miserably on the floor, I wasn't to stay there. He came to my arms which I lifted toward him, and these arms grew bigger in spite of my small size. They went from the back of my shoulders, over my shoulder blades, they were long, light, elastic, and they didn't end with hands.

My father's voice burst into rain on my face; my mouth open, tongue out, I absorbed the drops whose center was warm and whose outside was refreshing. It inspired me, it helped me no doubt: what contains all the vowels and begins with nothing at all? My brain was annihilated, I didn't even put the question to it. I didn't search for the secret of the enigma that the sunlight consumed at the heart of a vaster enigma, I had forgotten the bargain, the preliminary condition. I was so tense from determination I could have died. Seasons went by with the speed of minutes, centuries at the tempo of months. I kept crying: Papa pick me up! My own voice deafened me. My despair intoxicated me, I screamed: Why did you put me down? And at the same time I slid the answer into the question, his putting me down, which chopped my bones, having all at once filled me with such an unknown, violent, fortunate strength. I wanted. Let me go. Pick me up. Let me go. Pick me up. You will fall headfirst upward. I got a taste of fear. I used my flaming organs of sight. I was dying. I hastened to stand up to him. Henceforth I knew what I would always want in life: I would want to die upward and start over again from zero, along a line drawn from top to bottom to top. At the time I was five years old, and he was twenty-five, and T.t. was twenty but I wasn't his daughter.

Suddenly, amidst the flames that gnawed at my bones and my tissues without finishing me off, the pain ceased being mine and became my friend, my confidant, my mistress: it shifted with agility into a third body that extended between my father and me. I reflected it, I understood it, but I didn't contain it. I could have been anybody else, I was without name, without age, without sex, without knowledge. I was a memory lapse: I was remembering the question. And I had a sole objective: to go up, return to where I'd come from, up there. The pain didn't hurt me, the ignorance didn't scare me, I felt an unspeakable pleasure at sensing the elongation of these new arms whose lightness demonstrated that my old arms had been weighed down with hidden chains. I raised these arms that the wind carried. At once my body was drawn up, my right foot was vertical to the ground and my left foot was about to lift up when my cursed tongue—or maybe it was my soul made uneasy by this metamorphosis from its fleshly resting place—made me slip from blissful ignorance into the irremediable heaviness of knowledge. If I hadn't said at that point: A bird! *speaking of myself*, of *my* good strong wings, of *my* unbound body, lifted by the wind, I would have undoubtedly accomplished the eternal desire that generations of men have dreamed of. A bird doesn't know it's a bird: it knows only that the time has come to fly off, it does so, it doesn't think it, it doesn't say it. Therefore, I was not a bird. But the word had reached my father's ears, the total, well-hewn word. "L'oiseau." I was five years old, I won praise for my intelligence, the sunlight that fell across me resembled my father, who lifted me up to set me on his shoulders. I could have flown if I hadn't revealed the real secret. A trace of it remains, as T.t. knows: I'd almost have become an "O.S . . ." if I hadn't had this tongue in my mouth; and I've retained a very distant-close semblance to it, of which I'll speak later. But I was just the child perched on her father a short distance from the ground.

★

Eve would say during that time: all roads lead to Rome. And Rome is all places desired. Thus: one has only to depart in order to arrive. One has only to live in order to die. One has only to die in order to love and only to forget in order to start over. If I fall in the human manner I'm dashed to the ground, but the ground under the pressure of my desire dissolves and runs, and I cut through the groundwater, and if I push off, the ground fades and clouds over. Try it. Desire and you'll get it: you just have to desire strongly enough. Failure is only an experience. If you don't get to the point where infinity turns back on itself, it's because you haven't desired enough. Increase the effort. Do not speak. Words kill though they put no one to death. If you must have a language, let it be one whose quantity cannot be reduced to a single sound, one that moves without displacing, that describes without being written, that knows not the letter and yet is the spirit and has the spirit to be without recourse to visibility, that is made of time and not altered by time, that knows neither childhood nor age, neither the tongues nor the teeth that gnaw at foreign languages, that gives birth to itself, whose soul is everywhere and nowhere, that is free in its coupling. Air cut out of air.

This divine language would be common to all those beings—perhaps one, or two, maybe three—who have discovered the narrow bed in which opposites embrace, where heaven and hell unite, where extremes compose one tender visage to be absorbed into one another, where the egg can bring forth its own mother, where T.t. can be on my left while I'm nevertheless on his left, yet I see him glowing before my eyes at the same time I see his hair growing gray; then as I detach a smile with wings edged with a red border that has landed on my lips, my eyes see brown curls sprout over his forehead, and it's T.t., too, whom I nurse, I remember it, I had already nourished him two thousand years ago; and the cut air heats up because of the rapidity of infinity, for everything that lives so freely in the coupling is vivid and subtle like this wind which in a celestial season fecundates vultures in midair; and if only the motive force of infinity can increase some more, then all the air seized around the cut will resonate without any name ever being carved, nor any other word; only rivers reddened with the juice of poppies will flow into the ear, and the ear will no longer recognize itself, and continuing in this way, we shall arrive where the air cut out of air will erase all vestige of science and reason, where T.t. will be the cosmic Head [*Tête*] in the head, I his left eye and I his right eye, and the world will be music.

★

I didn't get down from on top of my father: I fell down. Voluntarily. I escaped from him and threw myself to the ground in anger. It seemed to me that even though the air had been refused to me, Nature couldn't refuse me the earth. I thus experienced the beginning of a pleasure in not feeling my movement thwarted. The laws supported me. The beginning is here the end: scarcely had I felt my chest sapped of exultation when I felt defeat fill my lungs with an abominable fire. I had chosen my hell: it was located at the exact point where birth and death overlap. To get there one had simultaneously to desire and to crush desire. Later I did this often.

What happened? My father having slowed my run by grabbing my ankle, I hit the ground on my head. My body slipped through his fingers, it was covered with that sticky film secreted by the infant just expelled. By the wound gashed across the bridge of my nose just between my eyes, I became aware of my blood, in my eyes and in my mouth. Seen through my blood, the sky seemed green to me and the earth was undeniably red and hot.

T.t. knows all this; he says that I came to the bird by going around the world, and that I look more and more like a bird. He says it with that smile that gives me a desire to fly.

After a night in which we crossed every realm making love, the bridge of my nose rips open in the same old place and streams with blood; one stream falls on T.t.'s chest, another falls on my chest. I explain to T.t. that the flow of blood is natural, since we've made love, that blood is my debt to nature, upon which T.t. asks me why I'm bleeding from the nose: would it be because my nose is the natural substitute for my vagina? Or for his penis? Now I'm worried. T.t. laughs, calls me a bird that's come back. But which bird? The one, he says, whose head is like that of a captor with an aquiline nose when he is Early [*Tôt*],* and the one whose wings are gold and purple when it's going to be *Tod*, and the one that resembles an immutable handsome young man when he writes, the One that resembles sovereign Egypt when the sun ceases to drink from the Nile and goes back into its shell. The one that keeps account of the dead and whose body is that of a king's son. The one that retains names and that serves language in silence and the sun with a trusty eye. It's a male during the day and in the Occident, at night it's the pale belly of the Orient, the mistress of tides, and the mistress of the mistress of tides. The waters are its slaves, births are obedient to it. And as T.t. is telling me of the loves of the Orient and of the Occident and how a quiver of the wings of the nose of Egypt armed and disarmed the fathers of the universe and how gold, gods, armies, laws, peoples, cycles, history, revolutions, prisons, science could dance like the earth around the sun:

I take him by the lips and by his tongue that is mine and I lure him toward another empire, beyond the unknown seas, I draw him toward the tree in Chile. So great is our joy at departing that my sides split, and the seven golden pleats that armor T.t.'s chest split, and from our cleaved body fall and roll particles of red glass, islands, continents, volcanos, panting as soon

*Here and elsewhere Cixous is punning with the word *Tôt*, "early," on both *Tod*, German for "death," and Toth, the Egyptian god of writing.—TRANS.

as they spew forth, golden entrails and sacred organs: finally the unique *solune,** which is sun when observed by man and moon when seen by woman. If I had sighted Chile by myself, I would have said that my voyage was cut from the cloth of dreams. If T.t. in my arms and his red unmoving lips under my lips and his forehead wreathed by my breasts had called me all the names of the Orient, I would have said it was part of Nature. But we were walking from the Orient to the Occident, with this rapid pace imposed on us by T.t., and which would have been that of the Gradiva if N. H. had given her his hand to pass from death to life. I love you in yourself and me in you. We had a single shadow the top of which touched the mountain *am andern Ende.* No one else was going by. Our walking gave rise to zones of shade and zones of sunlight.

T.t. asks me if I'd like for him to write my biography. At the time of our disappearances I would have detested being distanced from the book, I would have spouted out around us a bloody spray of suspicions. But now, when we were going to the tree in Chile, and when I looked more and more like a bird, I felt a great pleasure. It even *smiled* at me. Yes, the book was *this smile.* This Smile.

We dream but from the moment we have a single dream and a single body, consequently a single shadow and a single horizon, we are not dreamed: we bring to life or put to death our time under our footsteps. Seeing me-in-*Tod,* loved as-myself-in-Thot by T.t., I perceive that I am strangely free: I remember my father and Eve but the memory is not in *T.(ou)t.†* where I am, and I am not in the memory—I watch it pass by with the eyes of our third body. I did know it, it did have me in it, over there. Not here.

---

*A conjunction invented from the words for "sun" (*soleil*) and "moon" (*lune*). —TRANS.

†Play on T.t.'s name and the word for "all" or "everything" (*tout*).—TRANS.

And the lizard? He's dead. He's turning red. And my father? He was tall and supple and brilliant, green and gold. He was a curer of others, master of words, setter of things in their place, therapeutic, taciturn, he urged me to write, to count, to break up sentences with my ax to see what they contained, homeopath, carrier of children, short-lived. He went straight along the horizontal. He threaded his way among the rocks, he stopped in the sun, he moved about in the shade.

He went to bed Early (*Tôt*). He wanted me to imitate him.

★

Could you write our story? T.t. holds my hand. If I have time. How much time do we have? According to my calculations, we have nine centuries on one side, plus a dozen centuries on the other side. On which side? Our time has two sides: T.t. and I. We have gone through my side and our shade is still in front of us.

★

For the last time, we shall use today a borrowed language. Whether it's French there, or German here. And let's credit Pompeii for the nostalgia of my childhood, and let its ashes cover the head of the woman who smiled on me each time I could have flown away. T.t. brings me the green and gold lizard, oh my two distracted eyes and my two wide-open eyes! Have I already lost the sense of earthly color before the departure has even been decided on? Where was the green and gold lizard? I crossed Pompeii in twenty parallel journeys and twenty perpendicular lines. I squared it off into four hundred compartments, and I spent thirty more years in this desert waiting for it, in vain. I climbed mountains and I turned over stones, and I didn't see a green Sign, either high or low. Near the end of the last century I stopped. I had worn out my stick scraping rocks and digging between paving stones, and when I brandished it no bird responded anymore.

It's because the lizard was not in Pompeii, says T.t. I caught it somewhere else and at a time when you weren't born.

"It was there?"

"Not the green and gold lizard, but the *Lacerta Faglionensis* glistening among the rocks."

★

We are sitting on our bed in a shadowy temple without time. Outside it is noon. As it's a blazing noon on November second, only the dead are moving about noiselessly in the furnace, searching for their bones that neither the stars, nor the sun, nor the moon have gathered together, so that the bones of kings are mixed up with the bones of men. They will never succeed, says T.(ho)t., at getting their bearings because they have loved only the sun, the moon, and the stars and not the god who flows through the body of man.

★

By the will of N. H. the cleopatra butterfly was born. It was a slight wish, violent but modest, that's why what springs forth is the frailest nonhuman creature that can be born of man's desire. From Moses' rod a serpent could be born capable of killing priests and kings. The cleopatra is the Beauty of the German man's desire. Of my mother Eve's desire would undoubtedly be born the view of a long broiling street in the Orient, and she would stop before each stall to touch all the objects and desire them. What would be born of T.t.'s desire? Our immortality: he works time with the force of a Titan, in order to reverse it. We have already fashioned the place of our immortality: it is located at the intersection of both our desires stretched straight out, sprung from the same side of our silent united tongues, and, having fathers and mothers, origins and infinity, it appears all at once on the other side, in the form of a third body which in the mirror of my eyes is in his image which in the mirror of his eyes is in my image—in this body we are exchanged up to the last degree of resemblance; in this body we translate each other. What will be born of my desire? The unique and unknown body of our silence: we must find that wordless, limitless language that will perpetuate us without error and without weakening. Then carry out that flight that the word *Oiseau* suspended.

Today T.t. began making death go backward: "We rub out herewith the town where we were born, childhood memories, split rocks, cracked mountains, pillars supporting temples and separating armies, paternal kisses, mothers' waters, origins. We shall no longer need for Lizard to arise or for Sesame to open. In the cavern there is only the weight of things, the bags of gold and the bags of silver. Understand? The third body will pick up force and soul in what has never yet been seen; it will transport the over-there here; it makes the future now."

Today, November second, T.t. is beginning to push back our death. We need a lot of room for the hereandnow. Outside they're not unhappy. They calculate, they measure, they test, they've forgotten themselves, they've died without their names, without their eyes, without seeing themselves, four columns of clouds unfurl and swell toward the sky; there should have been only one, there was only one originally, but as a result of knocking against it blindly they burst it, and now the division process is incessant, the columns swell then burst, the clouds spread out, unfurl, rise, swell, then burst—Wake me, I say to T.t., I don't want to see that.

So he opens my eyes with such a joyous force that it's summertime. Not completely. It's a new season, or else an old one unknown to me: the budding flowers, the ripened fruits, the fragrances in boiling heat, are spread out among the innumerable folds of a blue cloak that I've seen somewhere before but that wasn't the same length as this one. This cloak is very long; it can, when unfolded, stretch out as far as the eye can see. When it is unrolled, the darker interior of the folds is revealed to be ocellated. The lining is made of a deep blue dried skin. The eyes that decorate the darker color are not men's eyes or those of any known animal; they attract the gaze of beings with or without souls, first by their luminosity; the source of the light is in the eye itself, which to me seems inconceivable. It works like this: each eye is an eye inside another eye. The second eye lights up the first eye. What astonishes me is that these eyes do not see, are not intended, in spite of their form, for looking. They shine, they've been created to receive images and not to reflect them. They are kinds of organic mirrors, analogous to the temple door that was not followed by any temple. They are absolute eyes, but I'm not sure about that. They shine too much for me to be sure of their color. It seems to me at times that their irises are on fire, hence glowing, but other times it seems to me they're made of ice. What are they?

T.t. says: I'd call those angels' eyes, they're anonymous eyes that don't reflect and simply gaze at the divine. In reality this tapestry of eyes that don't see is the celestial phrase.

"Where are we?"

"We are here. Absolutely here."

Here is our bed. Our third body stretches out there amid the silky red lands, sometimes I see myself, other times I see him stretch and unwind our limbs amid the lands of silk.

"Do you know that we are dead outside of death?" I nodded my head. My knowledge is entirely made up of a beatitude of all my senses and has no language, no name other than the impression of these lips that portion me out. I see through T.t.'s eyelids closed over my eyes a floating couple passing by who turn on a light for me:

"Do you know," I say to T.t., "that Dante actually went up to *look for* Beatrice?" T.t. knew. In his knowledge finally I eat the fruit of a happy sleep.

When I open my eyes, my milky eyes, I am sitting on T.t.'s breast and he's sitting under the tree in bloom. The garden where we are has four walls of water running vertically from bottom to top without any splashing. T(ou)t leans over me, his neck is long and graceful, his face has been set on fire by my lips, he sheds light on me to the point that I resemble him. He has this smile that I've seen somewhere before. He informs me that I have been born. I remember his voice: it gives us an infinite past. The nearby grows distant and returns with quick quivering movements that make his skin sparkle. He informs me that he has been born. That smile there. It is noon. *Il sole non si muove.* The sun is motionless. From here we see the earth revolve around the sun. We have stopped dying.

"Aren't you tired?"

"I have no body in which to be tired."

We know everything and yet we are innocent. We have no questions: over-there is but a reflection of here, the intersecting gleams of our eyes. T(ou)t then lays out for me all times;

I cry [*j'écrie*], I write [*j'écris*]; in writing a book is made that knows no times:* there is only one time. This time during which I write, am writing, is immobile, my writing hand is an eternity, my hand is so erect that the fingers are practically vertical. Under this vertical is inscribed a time without movement, without verb. Meanwhile, I'm writing with so much love and certitude, with that masculine force of the Red Sea when it brings down its broadswords on the army, the chariots, the pharaoh, and returns to its natural, perennial, closed, supple state, full of dead bodies, itself, that the book has no need of action, or verb, or movement. It winds up infinitely from the same point, in an eternal high-level present. I am the right and T.t. is the left, and this braided writing, conducted from left to right, tells a story without time, without history. Depicts rather a step. It (the writing) says "tu" to us, it gives us orders. It suggests to us to walk one in front of the other or one behind the other. But the right belongs to T(ou)t for I am the right, and because T(ou)t is the left, the left belongs to me, and we go across the writing with the same turning, rising motion, by means of our same third body, and I am the left and T.t. is the right; I see him move his right foot over the gap between two pages while his left foot prepares to follow suit; I write, I write till day springs forth from night. Then I write till night springs forth from day. If I had to give an accounting, I'd introduce this into the middle of a ring of doubt: I write at the order and from the dictation of T.t. At and from harass one another and I never know where we are. There are pages sprung from the day sprung from the night; there are pages sprung from the night sprung from day. Those from the night are shorter, clearer, heavier.

*Note that the word *temps,* here translated "times," can also mean "tenses."
—TRANS.

He dictates. I write. He reads. We then discover that there are three texts, the first, the intermediate one, and the second. The intermediate one flees and slips between night and day: at times I perceive its head, at times I take it by surprise at the moment its tail is still outside. All this to say that the nearby is far away, and even though I'm the one writing, I touch nothing, I steal nothing, on the contrary I lend. The rest is Nature. To begin, I write what comes:

Here where we are, the sun is vertically over T(ou)t's head, at the end of a straight line that bisects and holds the moon at the other end. We are equidistant from the Moon and the Sun, on the bed of air where I trim, row, plunge, tack, under T(ou)t's dictation, around the tree of disavowal. The tree turns slowly on its own axis; it emits in its rotation a natural music so heavy that at certain points the spiritual quality of this ponderousness affects the regularity of our metabolism. The breathing of Thote is accelerated to the point of moaning. This music can make us suffer, die, explode, revive. It seems to my ear that it's my heritage immediately transmitted to T.t. and intoned by a voice that once would have sung with words, but now is but an emptied bed, a dead throat nonetheless resonating. I am here caught up by the inconceivable, the unknown acknowledged, the violent grinding of these lopped-off, minced-up, immortal fibers; I understand that here there is not a music of the spheres but the rapid gasping of the infinitely regenerated demolition of matter. The tree pivots, pants, sweats, suffers or doesn't suffer; I want to put my arms around it.

When the moon is vertically over Tristan's Head, the Head seizes eternity. It works like this: first a patch of white curls grows; then a field of brown curls grows. The hair itself attacks time. Before my eyes T(ou)t transforms, he does it fast, he dictates to me faster and faster, a black strand falls on my forehead. Sad, tender eyes open all along the line traversing us by which we see everything at once. We are standing in front of the pomegranate tree, with eternity stretched out around us, though still not completely unfurled, without a wall, with no ground other than that which springs up at the slightest movement of our feet. Overturned temples pass by us, erected columns, empty stomachs, streams of stairways flow in the voice; no one passes, I recognize the pillar of Jeronimo by its vain rigidity and the rope tied around its capital. The moaning of the tree grows faster. I start: my guess is that this natural music that nibbles at the marrow of my bones comes from the chafing of death at the edges of life; if I couldn't distinguish it when my marrow recognized this music and moaned from its moaning, it's because it is the prenatal sound and the ultimate echo—it falters, it fades. The tree saws itself down. At the end of the sawing, there will be birth or silence. I lean against T.t.'s chest and he lays away my heart with his and lends to the vacillating tree his spinal column, then we take root with no difficulty. Here now. Reeds drag a river into blood. My Moses! What's he doing here? At the moment I cry, I break the last fiber, a torrent of tears carries my eyes abroad, T.t. hangs to a branch of the pomegranate tree that shakes off its fruit and falls flat on the ground. He is full of blood that came from where? I believe we are solidly rooted, but the universal silence is so urgent that we give in, having flowed one into the other. This silence will last. With red swords it tears down its walls around us. When one speaks in the water it can't be heard. We have nothing to say in any case, one bed's as good as another, one time as good as one time. No regret. My eyes? Milky eyes return to me.

"Are we in childhood?"

"No," says T.t., turning his fiery eyes toward my face, "we are above childhood, and we have flown here. The bed on which we're resting is a flat vessel with no limitations, a sky turned upside down, the blue cloak unrolled."

We watch the dance of the earth around the sun. They say it's a dance, but the dance is just the name of a comely threat. What we see is the original duel: here time is not yet cut off; it is not yet known which will engender which. All remains to be done. It is not yet known which will strike, which will open, which will enter, which will give birth, which will hide. It is known that this sight is unique. A purple silk cord ties the earth to the sun and separates the sun from the earth. The earth is far from us, as far away as the sun, but the rhythm of its dance gets into our limbs at the speed and with the gentleness of light. The rhythm is patterned on the phrase *Dig yourself in, the Sun will open up* [*Terre-toi, le Soleil s'ouvrira*], spoken as softly and as quickly as possible. The earth moves with the fascinating regularity of a pendulum, but very fast: so that this red mass that one might expect to see dance clumsily transports our motor nerves with pleasure because its oscillatory cadence goes at approximately three hundred sixty or sixty-five whole circuits per minute, thus more than four times faster than my body impulses. Such rapidity could have the inverse effect, give the illusion of extreme lightness; but it's not like that at all, fortunately: the earth moves unvaryingly from right to left to right, without this regularity suggesting any hidden clockwork. On the contrary, there is in this heavy, quick movement an animal power, menacing, promising: the result of the confrontation is unpredictable. A superb will animates the nonetheless fixed sides of the earth. A numerical relation ensures transmission of its movement to our blood. Very quickly our muscles resound to the tuning fork. What we see moving so far off with a mystical swaying gait is the earth's back: to be sure, the earth has no "back," but that's the movement made by the body, and this surprising, swaying gait gives definition to the mass.

It has stopped moving in a circle to go about in a narrow space only, with triumphant control. The purple cord resonates. Suddenly the earth is immense. I write: it's bigger. He says it's not any larger but appears to be because it's closer! And it's true. Without stopping its dance, the earth descends, pulling the sun which the purple cord causes to resonate. One senses here that the earth wants to kill. Its will comes over everything: it's that desire that weighs down on its sides. One senses also how deeply it loves what it wants to kill. It teeters at top speed so as to draw the sun toward it. If the sun hurls itself finally into the earth, they'll kill each other. Come, says the motive force, come. The sun is going down. What nuptials! How pure death is, how invisible, completely concentrated on the tautness of the cord—and death is its purple! More, more, more. What matters if everything comes to an end, if nothing is written anymore, and if the spirit is repudiated. The dance suffices. The fight. The music of death. So let it go on for three hundred sixty centuries and three hundred sixty-five centuries more and then nine times three hundred sixty-five centuries more. If need be. It must be. Then we shall come into our own. Now the sun is showing its big sad and tender eyes that my father left it. The earth holds us, stings us, tears us apart. One of the two lets out a cry: GET OUT of MY BOOK. T.t. says that it's the cry of the sun and that in fact it said: Get out of my bed! I say that it's the earth that cried: Get out of my book! Our accounts are the tree and the fruit.

We go out through the top, without using force, at noon and vertically. Between the opaque pillar and the luminous pillar which commemorate the dancers who are gone, the sky stretches out eternally and lawlessly.